Jail House Entertainment Presents:

"Struggles of A Made Man"

By: David A.
Feb. 17, 2006

1.8.07 Hey MOM, I'm Just chillin'
staying out of the way of

Acknowledgments

First and foremost I would like to thank
my higher power for blessing me with the
ability to write words with such
lucidness that they capture readers within
the first paragraph. Second, I would like to
thank my mother who has helped me
through my time of incarceration and
those who are considered family who
served time up at Coal Township with me
and helped me keep a level head.
Rob-Ar-, Troy, Sho, Zues, Sh8k, Na-Ack-,
And Spiz. I'd also like to thank all of you
that read this manuscript in its
raw form and gave their honest opinions,
(Good Lookin). It's funny to me cause
when you say "Crock" in Coal Township
you'd think of an athlete. Who would think
I could find time to write a book?
Finally I'd like to acknowledge my baby
brother Dwight. A-D- I love you man you
my heart baby boy...

Prologue

Life in the streets continue to change boys into grown men before their year. Although all aren't fortunate enough to see adulthood, Those that do would call themselves lucky. They are the ones who are victims of constant run-ins with crooks, crooked cops, and ruthless Judges. I'm an example of what the street life can do to a Nigga. The game was fair at first then shit got scarce and a nigga made a move that shouldn't have been made. I made a move with a nigga who was hard in the face, but soft to the touch. The pressure was turned up and he popped like a pimple. Me and my man went up for it, and although our time was cut short due to a technical reasons, I still managed to make moves, cause that's what a nigga like me do. We Hustle! I took some time to put it on paper so you could experience the game through my eyes...

<Philly's Deadliest Killah>

"Wake up! Wake up. Its time for you to go to court." said the C.O. I got up and washed my face then brushed my teeth. After getting dressed I looked in the day room to see three other people waiting to go to court. The news was saying it would be about 45 degrees out so I put on a sweater. I was thinking about my case and how much time I could face... Last month the DA offered me a 20 to 40, I laughed at that nigga and said. "You better start dividing by 5's or 10's before you start offering me something else!" Shit I wanted to go to court and pick twelve. But Lewis Delgado, my lawyer said, "You can't go to trial cause you have a statement against you from Lonnie." Lonnie and Terrell, two other niggas I was caught with at the shooting. Lonnie, a fine skinned young buck who was quick to rap, but quicker to shoot. He may not shoot straight but his point got across. They must of scared the shit out of him if that nigga talking I'ma put a bug in my man Tones ear to get at that nigga... Rell was a quiet nigga who was always plotting. That's why I fucks with him. Word on him was they used the good cop, bad cop shit and he stood strong. He was booked for possession with the intent to sell and possession of firearms with the intent to do bodily harm. Yeah, that's my nigga for life... Twenty-five to life if found guilty. My lawyer said snapping me back to reality. I focused and said. "That's if I'm found guilty!" I finished looking at him sternly.

"Look!" He said as his face hardened with seriousness. Then continued, "Your case isn't as strong as you think. Understand that even if your case has loop holes a statement pretty much sews them up."

"Hold up, can't we discredit that nigga or something? You know they say he was coerced into talking?" "I'll look into it, but in the mean time keep yourself out of trouble while I work on it..." The C.O. got on the mic and said," About five minutes and yall will be out!" sitting here I looked at these niggas, man they looked all excited and shit while I got knots in my fucking stomach. These are those same niggas you see on the street scrambling to get a hit! The door opened and when the C.O. walked in she was looking good as shit. I mean a nigga dick got rock hard quick. "Lets go gentlemen." she said softly. Even though she rocked a guard uniform, she made sure it accentuated her body. Ma had some nice ass thighs, and her hazel eyes stood the fuck out. All them niggas left first and I followed. When I walked up to her she smelled like raspberries. "What's up ma?" With a little smile on my face. She smiled with her full lips and said. "Aint nothing, is that a coogie?"

"Yeah, something small you know." I

looked at her name tag C.O. Cox.

"Cox, huh so do you have a first name?"

"Serena."

"So how often do you work?" I asked

"I work the night shift through the week and every other weekend."

"That's what's up maybe I'll holla at you tonight."

"I'm looking forward to it." she replied as she was closing the door... When we got to the bus that's where they put the cuffs on. I was getting on and I seen them niggas smiling, that shits crazy. I peeped Rell near the front and that's where I sat, by my man. "Sup my nigga?" Rell asked.

"Aint shit fam, what's the verdict with Mel (his supposed baby mom)?"

"Fuck that ho, Dog that bitch out there like a Chinese store open and shit."

"Damn dog. I thought she would at least ride, kid on the way and all."

"Nah, that bitch was lying. Probably wouldn't have been mine anyway!" Watching the road I reluctantly asked." What they saying about the case?" He looked at me and said,

"Shit aint looking good with this nigga Lonnie talking. I heard he might get time served."

"Damn!" I couldn't believe that. Rell looked back at me and said. "You know they gonna come at you with some bullshit, you gonna take it?"

"Fuck No! We can beat this shit if we get this niggas statement thrown out. The fucking witnesses' aint even showing up."

"I feel you, so what they charging you with?" He asked.

"Robbery and possession of a fire arm with the intent to bodily harm. They may throw the weapons charge out because they searched the car illegally. So if the witness aint showing up and we get this nigga statement tossed we walk." We hear a gate and looked out the window to see we finally arrive at the courthouse … When we got to the holding cell my lawyer came almost immediately and took me to a separate booth. " I have good news." He said with a grin on his face.

"Come on mother fucka fuck all that suspense, what's up?" I said becoming irritated. Before he spoke he showed me a sheet of paper. The top read, Lonnie Davenport found under the influence, and therefore his statement is inadmissible in court. Signed Judge Delricci... I couldn't hold back my smile.

"You know what that means?" Delgado asked

"Nah, won't you please elaborate?"

"They can't hold you due to the fact that there isn't anyone willing to testify against you and Terrell." He said with his usual bit of flare trying to sound all dramatic and suspenseful. "So how long until I can leave?"

"They may release you today if not they'll probably let you out later on tonight or tomorrow." He then got up and hit the button on the door and stated that he and his client were ready to approach the judge. He looked at me again and said, "Don't worry about the other $50.000, I got you off and by not seeing you again will be enough payment for me!" on the way back to the holding cell Rell was coming back with his lawyer smiling at me. I gave a little smile when I passed, after they took off the cuffs I sat down and started listening to them dudes talk about how they were getting money all over and like two hours passed and I had enough information to hit them niggas hard. I'll bet money that Rell was thinking the same thing. Niggas still say loose lips sink ships. I could hear doors opening outside the room; a C.O. came to the window of our door and called,

"Austin! Front and center." I stood and went over to the window, he then showed the cuffs.

"I need to take you to the Judges chambers." When I entered the room I could see the Judge. He looked to be I his late fifties or early sixties, with an Elmer Fudd looking ass face. I walked in and Delgado said,

"You don't need to say anything, ANYTHING!!"

"Aight" I said, the judge then asked me to have a seat. He and my lawyer started to talk, so I started scoping out the place. This nigga had a lot of plaques and medals hanging around. One of the medals said Congressional Medal of Honor. Another one looked like dog tags that said, Thomas Delricci <a.k.a. crows feet>. I laughed and they both looked at me. The judge asked me with a rather raspy voice, "Is there something you wish to share Mr. <he paused to look on a piece of paper> Austin?"

"Nah, my bad I was just reading your plaques and medals."

"I've lived a long life and I'm trying to help you do the same."

"So what's going to happen your honor?" trying to sound proper.

"You and your co-defendant will go back to your county jail and sign out sometime today or tomorrow." My lawyer stood so I did the same. After shaking the hand of the judge we took our leave. We didn't go back to the holding cell, we went straight to the bus were Rell was already waiting. Rell said, "It's about fucking time some good shit happen to a nigga for a change." I smiled and heard Delgado call, "Be sure to call me when you get home, aight." I just nodded and climbed the steps of the bus and sat next to Rell, and said, "You said it best my nigga...

Chapter 2

"Celly! A celly you know its chow time? I got your tray right here." I got up with a crazy ass headache. I brushed my teeth cause I could taste my shit was bangin: I looked in the day room and my celly held my spot in front of the T.V. He's a thorough nigga from G-town. He went by the name of Ant; I asked him what it was. "Mac & Cheese with fish and a thing of tea."

"Go head and knock that thing off I can't stand that fish" I said disgusted.

"Good lookin out. I went under my bed and grabbed a nutty bar. You know a nigga will eat something sweet fast as hell when he's hungry." I went down the tier to this nigga named Tommy cell and told him to give me his handle. Tommy was a gun out there in Norristown and I could use the extra hands if something pops off."

"What's the deal?" Tommy asked.

"Aint shit, a nigga got off and I'm trying to holla at you when you touch. So I'ma need your handle." he got up and grabbed a pen off his desk in the corner of his cell. The cell was decorated with bitches from the smooth magazine and a couple from XXL. Tommy, a dark skinned brother with a muscular build yet most would call him slow. He wrote his handle down and said,

"How you sleep through chow again?"

"A nigga was up all night, a when do you touch?"

"In about three months, just be sure to get at me you know these niggas get out and forget about people."

"Aight"

I said as I left his cell to jump on the phone. The phone was full plus there was some new dude on the phone. Hold up! This nigga was on the phone and he was just in the news for kidnapping little kids. This niggas a fucking baby chaser! I said to myself then made my way to the phone he had and said,

"Yo, I gotta make a call." He turned and looked at me; he looked like he led a hard life. His hair was dry and nappy. Clothes torn and sneakers old as hell and worn. My mind was racing, how these niggas let him on the phone? What's bad is this wasn't the first time he was booked for that shit. I wasn't going for that so I put a bug in my man Latifs ear. Latif was a nigga who was doing juvenile life and was quick to air a nigga out. I'm not gonna chance getting another charge, so I put my young buck on him. I told him I'll send him something when I touch. Little does he know I'm testing his loyalty cause I might have a job for him later. The phone was open and I got on and called my boo, Tanisha. She's dialed the number and waited to be connected.

"Hello?" she answered

"Yo what's up boo?" I asked happy to hear her voice.

"Aint nothing new, just worrying about you as always."

"I don't want you worrying yourself too much. Oh I'll need you to come get me later on tonight,

cause they letting me out."

"Why would they be releasing you did you make bail?" she asked.

"Nah, I beat my case!"

"Aah you did it, I can't believe it. I want to come see you!" She replied with excitement.

"You'll see me tonight. Oh do me a favor call Mel and see if Rell called yet. I'm trying to find out when he gets out."

"Aight...A crock, can I ask you something?"

"What?"

"Do you love me...?"

"Hello? Hello. Damn." The line went dead so I hung up. She gonna think I banged on her. I know she aint ask me did I love her! Fuckin phone cut me off again. I went to the C.O. on the block. Burns was working. We all called him Tex. Because of his size.

been riding with me since high school. I "A Tex?" I said

"Need something?" He asked as he turned to see me. "Who works tonight? Do you know?"

"It should be Cox the rotation doesn't change until the third." Today was Friday the first; I was heading to the cell when I heard my name being called.

"Crock! A Crock aint that that nigga that was tellin on yall?" I looked at the T.V. and the news was coming back on.

<Breaking News; one of the alleged shooters in the 19th street robbery was found dead in his Montgomery County prison cell. The name has yet to be released. But sources say it may have been a suicide. Police say with further investigation they will find the cause of death. We're going to you live at Montgomery County with Rachael Ming...>

"Hi I'm here with the deputy of this facility. Deputy, do you have any information at this time on the cause of death?"

"Through investigating this case we found that the inmate was under a lot of duress, due to testify against several mob bosses and a couple gang lords. we also found that both his daughter and fiancé were found dead in their home two weeks prior to his testimony. I wont say it was a suicide. Yet that is how it looks at this time..." "Thank you deputy! this is Rachael Ming live at Montgomery County We're now heading back to Sue with your local news."

"We'll be returning you to your regularly scheduled program. We will have more with this breaking story at 10:00. I'm Sue Sullivan and this is your Channel 6 news."

Jerry Springer comes back on talking about trailer trash hos sleeping with their fathers and brothers boyfriends. I couldn't help but have a little smile on my face. I went to the cell to chill and the C.O. got on the mic.

"Austin, your counselor wishes to see you." I hate that mother fucka. But I still went to see what the fuck he wanted. He was in his office with a cheap ass suit on looking like a white ass Urkel.

"Ah, Mr. Austin please have a seat." He said as he pointed to a chair.

"For what! How long you plan on keeping me?"

"Not long I just thought we could talk before you sign your release papers." His face started to ball with frustration. "Well I just need you to sign here, here, and here and I need your initials here on this line." As he pulled them out he showed were so I signed and initialed. He extended his hand and I looked at him like he was crazy.

"Fuck you pussy you thought I was the fuck guilty. You aint even give a nigga a chance." I turned towards the door and slammed it on my way out. I went up to my cell to relax for a while. I started thinking about Meme with her pretty ass green eyes. She got features of a Jada Pinkett with a fatter ass. I mean baby girl tight as hell. I keep picturing me sucking on those sexy ass titties. Not too big yet big enough for a mouthful...

Chapter 3

"Knock, Knock, Knock Dave? Yo Dave" as the voice continued to call. I know I'm just waking up but nobody calls me Dave up here. I rolled over to see it was Serena standing at the door.

"Yo what's up ma?" I asked as I sat up on the bed.

"Nothing, you wanna come out until your ride comes?"

"Yeah I'll chill with you for a bit."

"What you wanna watch?" she asked as she opened my cell.

"Whatever you watching." I got up and washed my face then looked out the door to see her walk down the tier. I wont front Ma got an ass like "Ester Baxter" and it looked soft enough to eat. When I was done brushing my teeth I grabbed my address book and left a note for my celly. {Holla if you need anything my number is (267) 253-3357. Everything in here is yours and the white boy Travis owes 20 soups and 10 bags of chips. That's you too collect.} I went down stairs and sat next to

Serena, she smelled nice I think it was cucumber melon or something. She had Belly playing when I asked.

"What time is it?"

"It's a quarter to one." she said looking at her watch, and continued with.

"Look fuck all the rap! You fucking with someone?" she asked with her soft voice.

"I wont lie to you, I've been with this one chic for a minute. She been pissed at me for like two

weeks, until she heard I was getting out."

"Damn, she sounds like a strong woman, yet how does she treat you overall?" she asked curiously.

"She rides but I never committed or anything like that"

"So what you sayin?"

"The doors open for your imagination. Take what you want from it and act!" I said looking back at the movie.

"So I wont have to worry about nothing if I gave you my address?"

"Hell no! I might even get you to move a few things for me if you willing."

"Depends on what you want moved, I don't want to get into any trouble or anything like that." she said looking concerned.

"Don't worry Ma. I got you just be ready to move when I call." I looked at her and smiled. she started to blush and said.

"What?"

"I'm trying to blow your back out sometime this week."

"Ooh, I like how your talking don't stop." she cooed

"Later these niggas could be ear hustling." She put her hand on my thigh and my man started to stand at attention. she started to lick her lips and I said,

"We could always go to the cell for a quick nut." I said watching her reaction.

"I can't let you fuck I just got to know you. I'll suck your dick though!"

Shit lets hurry up before they call you for your rounds." She got up and walked in front of me, I grabbed her ass as she was going up the stairs. When we got in the cell my pants were already down as she kissed me on the neck, then moved down my abs and kissed my navel. That's when I felt it; her lips were soft as rose pedals and warm like a summer day. I groaned a little and massaged the back of her head. She began to suck harder and harder like that of a vacuum. I started to think about fucking her with those big ass tits bouncing in my face. My balls started to twitch then I felt it in my stomach. I knew I couldn't hold back much longer.

"Yo I'm about to nut!" I tried to sit up but she pushed me back on the bed and sucked harder and faster, I let go and nutted in her mouth. She must have swallowed cause she aint do no spitting in the toilet. She got up and fixed her hair then said, "That's a little taste of what you'll be getting later." I got up to fix my gear when the phone rang. She was already down the stairs then she answered.. All I heard was okay then she started her rounds. When she came to my cell she said, "When I'm done I'll let you out cause your rides here."

"Around what time do you want me to call or come over?"

"Anytime after twelve-thirty" I went down stairs and waited for her to let me out. When I got out front Meme was waiting for me with her girlfriends Grand Cherokee.

"Crock!" she yelled as she ran up towards me then jumped into my arms. I kissed her on the cheek then she asked,

"Have you had anything to eat?"

"Nah, I wasn't hungry plus I wasn't feeling that well."

"Do you want me to stop anywhere?" she asked, "Nah, take me home so I can take a shower. I feel dirty." as we pulled up to my place she looked at me and asked,

"Can I come up with you?" I wont deny my baby girl access to the crib so I told her she didn't have to ask. She made her self comfortable by turning on the radio then sat on the couch. I got right in the shower, while in there I started to think, I know I got a dick suck, but she could have been out and about too. Damn I don't even trust someone whose been riding with me for like six years. I could feel a small draft and I looked through the pane glass on the door.

The door slid open and she was standing there in a towel, "Can I join you ?" she asked.

"I thought you were never coming." she dropped the towel and revealed her nice pert tits and tight body. She only stood at 5 foot 2 inches so I helped her as she stepped in. She kissed me on the chest and wrapped her arms around my neck. I kissed her and grabbed her by her tight round ass and lifted her up. As I entered her she let out a loud yelp and wrapped her legs around my waist. "Make love to me David." She whispered softly. I continued to thrust and lift her back up off my man. I started to suck on her neck and felt my legs get loose. I placed my hand on the wall for a little support. She started to moan louder and her breathing grew more rapid. I could feel her pussy start to contract on my dick, that's when she scratched me on my back and whispered, "I'm cummin, I'm cummin, oh my God I'm cummin!" when we finished she did something I've always loved. She kissed me on my bottom lip. It's so sexy the way she's so seductive after such intimacy. She stepped down and said, "I know you love me, you're just afraid to admit it!" I looked at her and she was looking even more attractive. I thought to myself could I truly love this woman? I finished washing up and dried off. When I went into the bedroom I had my boxers on. I looked at the bed and she was already snuggled in. I said fuck it a nigga gotta sleep. I checked the alarm clock 4:38 am. Damn I forgot to call Rell. I made a mental note to call him tomorrow. When I got up under the covers she turned towards me and put her arm around my chest, I slowly went to sleep...

Chapter 4

I woke up to the smell of eggs and sausages. The bed was empty on the other side, yet it was made none the less. I went to brush my teeth and look in the mirror.

To see my reflection had me thinking, (when was the last time I woke up and had someone else cook in my house?) Man I might have to slow down, she acting like a trooper but she might be stunting. Shit I know the rules to the game played, I can't leave my man hanging like that... The steam from the water fogged up the mirror, I wiped it off and went to get dressed. I put on my Roc-a-wear jeans and a white-T. I slipped on my air force ones and went to the kitchen. I slowly walked in to see Meme washing a pan. The table was set with two glasses of orange juice and two plates of French toast, sausages and grits. I looked back at Meme and leaned on the door, to watch her work for a while. She was dressed in one of my T-shirts that went to her ass. I thought to myself how long would this last? She turned around with the frying pan and dropped it when she saw me.

"Shit, you scared the hell out of me!" I walked in and sat down. After hanging the frying pan she came over and kissed me on the neck.

"Rell called you at like 8 o'clock.

"I'll call him later." I said as I started to eat. "You not gonna go and get into some kind of trouble are you?" she asked

"No why you hounding me like that? I just got out yesterday."

"You better stay the fuck out of trouble! I mean it." angrily speaking.

"Aight damn can a nigga eat?" Agitated I finished and washed my plate and glass. I picked up the phone and called Rell.

"Hello" Rell answered.

"A you busy?" I asked

"What the fuck! I called earlier and Meme answered. You gonna make her wifey aint you?"

"I don't know she definitely plays her part." I said looking at Meme.

"So you tryin hit the block?"

When Rell asks to hit the block nine times out of ten he wants to feel someone out and plan our next moves.

"Yeah meet me at Italiano's."

"Aight, One."

I hung up Meme was washing her plate when she looked at me.

"What I do now?" I asked with content.

"Can you promise me one thing?" she asked as she put the plate up.

"What?"

"Promise me you won't get yourself killed out there cause it would hurt me so much."

"Come on wi..." as I was cut off she said,

"I don't think I could make it without you again!"

"I will promise to always be careful while I'm out there, cause God knows my time." I looked at my watch ten minutes to twelve. "I gotta go, come here and give me a kiss!" as she did it I grabbed her ass and told her I'll be back around like four. "Call me if you need a ride or some money."

I went outside and remote started my Infinity Q45. That's my baby, all cream with smoke 20 inch Savini rims. Special smoke tint with four T.V.'s in her with a navi. I drove around the ave for about ten minutes then went to Italiano's. The ave. is always packed on Saturdays, especially at noon. I had the front window down about half way and I had that pac shit slamming through the 15 inch autobahn subs. I see nothing but heads turning, the light turned red and I slowed to a stop. I could see Italiano's up on the right and I could make out the tail of a gray maxima. It must have been Rells. He had a 2000 max that was gray with black trim. He had 20" chrome spinners on it with the windows tinted on it to the point of being black.

"Honk, Honk, lets go motherfucka! Green means go!" I looked in the rear view and seen this young nigga talkin shit out of his celebrity. I got out the car and my hoodie swung open. He must have seen the butt of my .45 cause he sat back and got quiet. I went to this nigga door and asked, "you got a problem living?" I snapped and continued with, "cause the way you talking, makes me think you don't have an interest in living." "Nah, I aint mean nothing by it. I was just in a hurry my bad." I started back to my car watching this fool cause you never know what a nigga thinking about. He then drove around me and turned left. I went up a little and parked behind Rells Maxima. As I got out of the car some young chick approached me and said, "Hey good lookin what you bout to do? Cause a sista tryin to holla."

Shorty wasn't bad but she had braces that made her look foreign. She had the slanted eyes and nice long silky hair. Her body was nice but I had something better at home.

"What's your name?" she asked with a little lisp.

"Crock, look ma, I hate to turn you down but I got business to handle."

"Well let me at least give you my number."

"Aight" I watched as she wrote Renee (215) 848-7421.

"I'll holla at you later ma."

I looked at her walk down the street and her ass looked like a pillow was stuffed in her pants. I walked into Italiano's and seen Rell in a booth by the window.

"You done?"

"The fuck you talking about?"

"I'm talking about you and them hos you keep talking to." He looked serious about what he was Saying.

"Yo, what the fuck you getting at with all this?" I asked. "My bad dog I know you got a rider at home and they still want you."

"That's it dog, they want what they can't have!" I put the number on the table and looked at him.

"Here dog, I don't want you to think I don't appreciate Meme, cause I do. Shit a nigga may be in love!"

"Damn you serious huh? That's what's up" as he took the number I wanted to know something.

"What we gonna do about them niggas Link and Boo you had beef with before the shooting?" watching for his reaction, But couldn't find one, His face stayed plain which meant he was thinking, He looked up at me and asked.

"Don't they hang out in that old crib behind the lounge?"

"Yeah why?"

"Let's call Dex up and have him meet us at the lounge." Rell pulled out his side kick and took another swig of Yac out the bottle. MY phone rang and when I looked at the caller I.D. it said home.

"Hello", I answered.

"Crock where you at?" She replied. "I'm at Italianos, why what's up?"

"Melanie came and got the truck cause she had to go to work. So I'ma need you to drop me off at work tonight."

"What time you gotta be there?" I asked while looking at my watch 2:30, pm she said.

"I gotta be there by four o'clock."

"Aight, I'll pick you up in about an hour."

"Crock?"

"What's up?"

"I love you." Then she hung up. Damn, I couldn't even comment, she thought she was slick. Rell finished his call and said "He gonna meet us there in about five." "Aight, look we aint gonna run right up in there cause word is they got lookout boys on them roofs, we gonna have Dex go in there and tell them you were in the bar."

"Why the bar?" Rell asked.

"Cause Stan runs that shit and he'll clean up for us. Aight?"

"Aight," Rell responded. We drove to the lounge and I went to holla at Stan. I told Rell to holla at Dex to set it up and wait for us outside after they enter. "You gotta stop drinking too!" I said. After talking to Stan he said "Listen up young blood, set your meeting up while were empty."

"Aight." As I listened I went to the back of the bar where there was a walk in booth. I sat in the back corner and waited, and then Rell walked in with Dex. Dex was a young nigga known for clapping that heat. He's a true gun and he rides for me when I need him. That's the nigga I had running shit behind Rell when I was in New York. I see Dex go back outside and Stan turned the lights down. Rell still had that bottle of Cognac looking drunk as hell. Dex came back in and said "What it be Crock?" he asked eagerly.

"Yo you get filled in?"

"Yeah, when you want me to do this?"

"Right now and when they come in stand in front of the bar by my car cause something might pop off!"

"Aight" He left the bar and as he was leaving he unbuttoned his jacket...

Chapter 5

In walked Linx wearing a black Fubu hoodie and black jeans. Boo came in rocking a white T and some blue jeans.

"Sup, Crock?" Boo asked. Before I could respond Rell said

"Sup?! Naw nigga what the fucks up with you?"

"What you aint got no time for your friends no more?" Boo replied as they sat in the two available seats in the booth.

"The fuck outta here!" Rell said and continued with "Nigga we aint never been friends!"

"Look", Linx cut in "We aint here for no bullshit, we came to talk." I couldn't read these niggas so I said. "Talk, Talk about what?"

"We heard what happened to your team." Linx said. "Shame, a damn shame." Boo slid in and cutting him off.

"And your point"! Rell said with a slur while waving his yac.

"And Linx said calmly, we wanna make you an offer."

"Listen man, y'all aint got nothing I want." I said with my patience beginning to dwindle.

"Come on nigga" Boo said "We know what happened to them niggas, it's a rap for them!" He looked at Rell then back at me with a grin and continued "You, me and Linx can make some shit happen. You may not need money but we do."

"Hold up a minute." Rell said angrily spilling his drink."

"Crock always been his own man, so what my team gone. That aint stopping me from shinning." Rell said as he stood to leave. As he finished he tried to walk away, but Boo wasn't finished. "Hold the fuck on!" Boo said grabbing his arm. "We aint finished wit..."Before he can finish his sentence, Rell smashed him in the side of the head with the bottle of cognac, Boo stumbled and fell head first by the bar.

Rell followed up with a swift kick to the ribs sending him falling through the front door.

"Is you fucking crazy?" Rell yelled. Linx managed to pull his Glock while his man was getting his ass whipped. He was trying to creep Rell to end his life, but changed his mind when the darkness exploded with flashes of gunfire. I was spitting at theses niggas to free my man up. On the way out I seen Linx duck behind a car and Dex walked over and started busting at Linx then took off in his Denali. Boo took one in the head and fell immediately. Rell was so angry he kept kicking Boo not realizing he was dead. I knew he was out of it cause he was bleeding from the hand and seemed to pay it no mind. I grabbed Rell by the arm and he followed up with a right hook. I managed to slip most of the blow but he still caught me on the chin. He continued by grabbing his hammer with his left hand. I rushed him and ducked under his shooting arm. I grabbed him by the waist and tried to toss him and failed. So I pushed him a little and when he tried to fight back I flipped him about three feet which made him drop his P89. He rolled over and looked up, he must have been embarrassed cause he pulled a dagger from his boot and started to charge. I thought and quickly came to the conclusion. I'd have to shoot my man to prevent any injuries to myself. I pulled my .45 and started to create space between us. Dex pulled up behind me with Melanie and Tenisha. They got out and Meme screamed.

"Rell! What the fuck you doing! I know you aint about to get at your man!" Rell stopped and looked at me, I mean really looked at me then looked at Meme. "Meme?" He said looking back at me and called "Crock?" He looked like he couldn't understand what was going on. He dropped the dagger and started to whimper. Stan came out and said. "Y'all better get the fuck out of here before the cops come." I helped my man up and put him in his car with Mel. Me and Meme got in the car and took off to her job. While in the car Meme started punching me in my arm.

"What the fuck you trying to do, get put back in prison?" She hissed angrily. "No baby girl, those niggas got us booked in the first place. They tried to take our strip so we deeded them niggas."

"You better not be hurt, Dex told me you were in trouble so I came as quick as I could." We pulled up to her job and she kissed me on the cheek. "Pick me up at midnight, Aight" "Yeah." before she got out she looked at me and said, "you know I love you right, Don't be getting into trouble while I'm at work I mean it!" The look she gave meant she was serious.

"I Won't" I went to the spot and watched them niggas finish the product for about two hours. I rolled a blunt and went back to my car. I got in and rolled to Rells crib. Rell lived up Broad and Olney on 13th street. He has a nice little spot where he and Melanie stayed. I brought up on occasion about moving. I went to his door and knocked rhythmically.

"Who is it?" Asked a soft voice I recognized to be Mel.

"Crock"

"Hold-on" I heard a click and a chain sliding then it opened.

"Hey crock, Rell is in the living room."

"Aight"

The house smelled like chicken. When I went in I seen Rell with a big ass piece of chicken in his hand.

"Sup fam?" Yo my bad about earlier today."

"It aint about shit we family. What you doing?" I asked as I flopped on the sofa. "Checking the news cause I might have to bring the dog in." Referring to Onyx in the backyard. She's a black and white pit with a blue eye and brown eye. He loved this damn dog. "You love that damn dog, It's no wonder you aint got a wifey. She out back." I laughed at my slick remarked and looked at Rell, this nigga had chicken every where. This nigga looked commercial. I couldn't stop laughing. Then Mel said; "You got jokes nigga?" Looking angry.

"Nah" I said still laughing.

"You right, I got you, you a motherfucking comedian now. Huh?" Rell said as he wiped his face off. "Nah, Nigga you just funny as hell!" Mel walked over to Rell and asked

"Can you take me to the movies? I wanna see the new Denzel flick." "What time does it start?" Rell asked.

"About Ten O'clock." She responded.

"What you doing tonight Crock?" He asked as he wiped the table.

"I gotta pick my girl up at midnight."

"Your girl?" Mel said quizzically. "So you asked her out?"

"Nah, not yet I was thinking about asking her tonight. Shit she rode with me this long".

"Shit y'all way past boyfriend and girlfriend." Mel replied.

"Hold up I'm just asking her to ride not be wifey, stop assuming shit all the time."

"Why don't you call someone up and roll with us to an early movie? " Rell interjected. Mel looked at him with a crazy look, and then snapped at him. "You aint' no fucking good!" "What? You wanted to go to the movies he might as well come too." Rell pleaded his case. "Shit, he aint gonna go by himself is he?" "Don't worry about it maybe we could all ride together tomorrow." I said trying to kill the argument. "You sure?" Rell asked. "Yeah, I'll go check out a club or something." Rell looked like he was trying to figure me out.

"Aight then." I got up and left and when I got in the car the radio had on the weekend mix off. I said fuck it and put the blueprint on when the car got warm and drove to Jersey to hit P3. P3 was a club for semi-Ballers. The women be deep and it's a good spot to chill. Niggas don't be on any bullshit. Plus stretch is a friend who played football with me in school. Once I arrived I left the guns in the glove compartment and went in the club and found an open table and sat down. Stretch came walking up to my table.

"What's crackin my nigga?" he said with excitement .

"Aint shit playboy, how's the club?"

"Making money as always, but look I need a favor."

"You know I just got out and I'm not looking to go back this soon either." Knowing its nothing good he's about to ask.

"I can dig it. I just heard there's some nigga going around cleaning up on some people's strips."

"I aint hear about it."

"You're hearing now nigga I know you heard about Linx and Boo?"

"Nah what happened?" I learned never to tell this nigga anything cause he'll talk with no pressure.

"They got gunned down in front of Stans lounge."

"Damn!" I hope I aint gotta shoot this nigga, I said to my self". "They know who did it?" I asked.

"I haven't heard who did it, but that nigga older brother is the one who cleaning up."

"What's his name?"

"I also heard th..." cutting him off.

"You heard a lot didn't you?"

"Yeah, but it looks like five of these niggas and they already took over Sanchez's and Titos' strip. They trying to lock down the city." He said sounding concerned.

"As long as they leave my shit alone, they'll be cool."

"You still single aint you?" he asked.

"Yeah, why you wanna know?" concerned I asked him.

"Chill! I got this new girl, sapphire who's dying to meet you." He gestured and she walked up wearing a one piece that only covered her nipples and pussy. Her titties swung as she stepped up to take a little spin for me. As she turned I could see she had a fat ass cause her thighs were thick as hell. After she spun she sat on my lap and began to gyrate her hips.

"I'll let you two get acquainted." He said as he left. She was good at what she did cause my dick got hard.

"Oh, I see your enjoying this." She said acknowledging she could feel my man.

"You good" I responded.

After a couple minutes she changed positions. She laid back on me and spread her legs, I know she felt me now but she kept going. I grabbed her to make her stop. She aint gonna give me blue balls. She was smiling as she got up.

"Maybe later we can relieve you of that?" as she looked down. I looked at my watch 10:30 I had to go get Meme, if I leave now I'll get there at about 11:30. I told sapphire.

"Tell stretch I'll see him later and I'll look into his favor!" I peeled off $300 and gave it to her then left the club...

Chapter 6

The clock said 11:45 and I sat outside Memes job. she worked as a registered nurse at the mercy hospital. I was watching scar face on DVD when I looked up at the front doors. There seemed to be little movements inside. The movie ended and I put on the radio, there was some slow jams playing. Tamia "There's a stranger in my house" came on. I reclined the chair and closed my eyes. After a couple songs I felt myself falling to sleep. I cut the car off and locked the doors, then laid back again. Tap-Tap-Tap! Startled I jumped up with my.45 in hand.

"It's me! Put that shit away. I can't believe you!" Meme yelled.

"What! Shit you scared the hell out of me."
I holstered the gun and opened the door.

"Here baby you drive"

As I got out the car I gave her the keys.
She unlocked the door and I got in. after
putting on my belt she kissed me and
asked,

"You miss me?"

"Yeah like hell"

"You were asleep how long you been out
here?" she asked as she pulled from the
hospital.

"Since 11:30" as I got comfortable I closed
my eyes again.

"You wanna go to my house tonight?"

"Yeah, I don't care I just need some rest."
On the way my phone began to ring.

"Hello?" I answered still feeling the effects
of being sleep.
"Yo what's the deal?" asked Dex.
"Aint shit, what you need?"
"You aint hear?! Some nigga named
Kendal up here trying to clean up on a lot
of paper. Plus word is he looking for some
niggas to bring in his brothers killers."
"Oh, well just lay low for a while."
"Nah, nigga I killed that nigga I'ma find

him and box that nigga dog that's my word. Aint no one gonna catch me slippin." Dex sounded more agitated than angry.
"Yo do what you gotta do, but don't get caught being stupid."
"Aight"
"Call me if you need me." I then hung up the phone.
"Who was that?" Meme asked
"Dex..."
       On the other side of town Dex was already strapping up for war. He was a smart nigga, hence the name Dex. Once he got his shit together he loaded up the Denali. He may have been a bit excessive; he had two 9mms with silencers and two P89 Rougers. He also loaded two Uzis and a AK47. He wanted to hurt them niggas but lacked the man power. He hadn't the time to call around so he left. He caught word Kendal was gonna be at this nigga Pete after hour spot. Pete was cool with him so he knew he was in. after a ten minute weed break. He lost the edge and rolled out. It took him about twenty minutes to arrive at the spot. He noticed niggas getting patted down at the door and Pete was out there. He figured he'll take the chance and see if he could use his friendship to bypass the pat search. Getting out he walked right up to the front of the line to Pete.
"Pete? Were you been hiding, what's up?" in his best impression of himself.

"A Dex how you been?" giving his man a dap.

"How's the party coming?" Dex asked as he looked inside.

"its aight, you coming in?" there's always room for an old friend."

"Yeah, hold up though." Dex pointed to his waist. "I gotta drop something off." Pete nodded and Dex ran to the car, he put the silenced nines in his holster and left the rougers then headed back. He and Pete walked in together but Pete was pulled away by one of his hostesses. The club was jumping but Dex was focused on finding Kendal. He continued to look around and seen he was sitting at a table with three bitches and two other niggas. Looking around for a lookout guy, but none could be found. Dex slowly made his way around the back of the table where he placed the silencer on his 9mm. one of them niggas he was sitting with left towards the bathroom. With him two of the to hit one of them niggas. He followed him to the bathroom, when he entered there was a person pissing but it wasn't him. Dude finished and left and Dex locked the door seeing there were two stalls and one out of order. He knew where to find his man. Standing in front of the stall he kicked the door in and let three shots fly. Two to the sternum and the last in the head. As he closed the stall door he put tissue in between the crack to keep it closed. When he unlocked the bathroom

door he wet his hands and left after drying them. As he went back to scope them out he felt a bit of excitement. As he got back to the middle of the floor he watched for about three minutes then Kendal leaned over to his man and his hommie got up and hustled towards the bathroom. Dex couldn't believe how easy this would be. He followed and grabbed his nine, when he walked in the thug said,
"The bathroom's off limits," And pulled out his cell while walking towards Dex. Dex pushed him back with his left hand and raised his gun.
"Holla at you on the other side mother fucka!" and shot him four times in the chest. The door opened and Dex played like it hit him in the face, keeping his identity masked he rushed to the table and sat down with Kendal, startling him.
"I heard you looking for them niggas that killed your brother!" staring at him blankly.
"Yeah, you know something about them?" Kendal asked. Dex played it off smoothly.
"Yeah I got their pictures right here."
It appeared he was going in the coat pocket but grabbed his hammer and shot five bullets into Kendal's lungs. As soon as he shot him screams came from the bathroom and it erupted through the club and over the music. People began to run out and Dex jumped into the crowd with them. When he got to his Denali he felt relieved. He drove off and was going a bit

fast but he was coming off a high. Then that's when he seen them. The blue and red lights of a Police car. Dex pulled over and grabbed his nine. He looked to see how many cops there were through the rear view. One, good he put his information in his left hand and aimed the gun through the door.

"License and registration please?" asked the officer. As soon as he reached he said "going a bit fast..." but was cut off by the three shots the hit him in his crotch. Dex opened the door and pulled his other rouger and was met with four bullets. Two hit him in the stomach and two hit him in his chest. Dex responded with two shots to the cops face and climbed back into his truck. But only made it about a hundred feet from the cop where he fell to the steering wheel... Beeeeeeeeeeeeep...

Chapter 7

I woke up to the sound of my cell phone ringing. Meme was still sleeping soundly, so I got up and went to the bathroom to answer it.

"Hello?"

"Yo what's the deal nigga?" the voice said

"Who the fuck is this?" I snapped not recognizing the voice.

"Yo its Ant, nigga your celly!" he sternly responded.

"Oh, what time is it?"

"Like eleven thirty, Yo I called cause "TIF"

said you had something for him.
"Where he at?"
"He in the hole he stabbed some pedophile, damn near killed him. He said to give you his name Thomas Williams, so you can get at him."
"Aight Good lookin. Yo you tight up there?" I asked concerned.
"Yeah I'm straight. I'll get at you later."
"Aight holla back."

I made a mental note to take him $300 today. I went into the bedroom and kissed Meme on her nose. She looked up and kissed me.
"I gotta go. Call me later aight." She nodded and got back under the covers. On my way home I put on the news and they was saying, <another tragic incident occurred last night a 3:30 there was a shooting at an after hours spot on 17th and Susquehanna ave. three were found dead in the club, and ten minutes from the shooting an officer was found shot to death. The apparent shooter was found inside a black Denali with four gunshot wounds of his own. The officer is survived by his wife and three children. Our regards go out to his family.>

I couldn't believe this shit. Dex went on a shooting spree. I wondered who got shot in the club. After the news went off I put a CD in then I pulled up to my place and got out, I was going to take a shower but thought I'll be hollering at Serena later on. When I went in I locked the door and threw my keys on the counter. I went straight to the bathroom and started my shower. As I finished I cut the shower off to hear my phone ringing. I grabbed a towel and ran to answer it.

"Hello?"

"What it is?" Rell responded.

"I just got out the shower."

"Oh, word on the street is Dex killed some nigga named Kendal and some cop."

"Yeah I heard, shit was just on the news."

"A bad way to go but the only way if you ask me!" Rell spat

"Yeah he a true warrior, look I'ma get at you later cause I gotta get dressed."

"Aight I'm going back to bed, holla at me later."

Once I got dressed I took $2500 out of my pit bull statue in the living room. I grabbed my keys and headed to the county, on the way I picked up some Mickey D's. Once I got there I put three hundred on Latifs books and two fifty on my celly books. On my way out I bumped into this nigga I know from school. I only knew him as "D", I never asked his name. he recognized me from what it seemed.

"Yo what's the situation?" he asked giving dap.

"Aint shit, you know me maintaining." He had a nice young thing with him and I waited to see if she was with him.

"Oh this my man "J" girl. I see you looking. You know "J"?"

"He from G-Town aint he?"

"Yeah, he'll be out in a month." "D" said
"Look this man number, you still at the
top of your game?"
"Yeah I still dabble." He said.
"Where you play ball at now any way?" I
said cunningly.
"I get my rec in at CHI town nowadays. I'm
staying in a motel in center city for a week
though."
"Call that number and set up a meet. My
man will drop you something off that'll be
good for the business."
"Aight what you looking for?" he asked I
leaned in and whispered.
"I'll give it to you for 32 a key, so give him
800G's."
"Aight good lookin."
As I left I remote started the car when I got
to the parking lot to think...
         Woof, woof, woof, the dog continued
to bark non-stop.
"Aah damn dog!?"
"Why you yelling so loud" Mel asked as
she rolled over to her man.
"Fucking dog keeps barking." Looking at
the night stand Rell realized he over slept
his first appointment. Grabbing his cell he
called up his buyer from D.C. named "E".
"Talk to me" replied the voice.
"Yo its your one o'clock ." Rell said in a
humble voice. "I overslept and I'm still
looking to see if you can baby-sit?"
"Yeah I got room."
"I got two fourteen year olds at 33 a head."
"So that's about nine hundred and twenty

five, huh?"

"Yeah same as always."

"Aight"

Rell liked dealing with "E" cause he was always good money. Plus they been working together for about three years.

Ring-Ring his phone rang in his hand.

"Hello?"

"Yo this "D" from CHI-town, Crock told me to call you to set up a meet for twenty five pound puppies."

"Where you wanna meet at?" Rell asked

"At 69th street terminal, I'll have a bulls cap on."

"I'll have a 76re's hat on.

"Aight how long will it take?" "D" asked

"Give me an hour and a half."

"Aight"

Now Rell was eager to make the drop with "E" cause he hated to be late and he's a major mover for Crock. I can't fuck Crock business up by being late to his buyers, he relied on me. As he was washing his hands and face Mel came in and said,

"When you come home I got a surprise for you."

"Aight just remember to bring the yac."

"That's all you think about your precious cognac or alizae." Mel hissed

"You need to think about me like that." She said mugging the back of his head.

"Come on baby you know you'll always be my number one drink." Rell responded as he put on his coat.

"Come over here and give me a kiss and stop trippin'." She complied and Rell grabbed the keys to his rental and drove to the corner of 52nd street. He recognized "E" and they did their little act. Shaking hands and switching their sets of keys and parted ways. Rell turned the Chevy on and drove to 32nd street to drop off four hundred grand. He then smoked a couple blunts and let an hour go by. He went to drop the rest of the money off at 17th street...

You know what fuck it, I decided to check on Onnie, Blaze and Byron. Blaze and Byron are some shaky niggas who run my product on 17th street and Onnie push on 23rd. every time Byron run my shit there seem to be complaints about the product. I pulled up on 17th street and all them niggas were there, that's good I said to my self. I'ma let these niggas know I aint playing with my money. I grabbed the bat out of the back seat and rolled up on them.

"What's up fellas?"

"Aint shit." Blaze said "out here grinding."

"Aight so how we looking?"

"Everything good on my end Boss!" Onnie said handing me his wad of money. "That's good money Crock he finished."

"Aight" I said while thumbing through the money.

"What about you Byron?" I asked flipping the bat from left shoulder to right.

"I got eight for you now and the rest when it's finished." Byron said nervously.

"Yall niggas aint done yet?" I asked looking at them niggas.

"Shit my peoples done!" Blaze said handing me his money. Then finished with , "you know I come on time every time!" I smiled and said,

"You still my nigga" throwing dap, and then I took the tribute "oh you check on that for me Blaze?"

"Yeah"

"And the verdict?"

"Bogus as hell!" Blaze said shaking his head.

"Damn can't win em all. Yo Byron!" I yelled as I switched the bat back to the left shoulder.

"I'ma only ask you once. You switching my shit with yours?"

"What?!" Byron said startled. "Hell nah Crock"

"I think you lying to me. See I set your punk ass up. I wasn't even gonna follow up with it but there's something about those complaints that nagged me. That's when it hit me." I said switching the bat back to my right shoulder.

"They only seem to come when you on shift!"

"Nah" Byron said backing up "I wouldn't try you like that."

"Bullshit!" I said and punched him in his mouth. Byron staggered but stayed on his feet.

"You a crab ass nigga Byron and I'ma fix your problem today! Trust." Byron's eyes grew big then he tried to plead.
"Wait Crock, I got your money I swear." Without hesitation I swung the bat which whistled through the air. Byron tried to duck but was too slow. All that was heard was a sickening crunch, blood splattered on Onnie and Blaze as Byron's skull caved in. This nigga was twitching like a fucking bug as I followed up with another blow that ceased his movement.
"Bitch ass nigga. A, you two clean this shit up!" I snapped as I headed back to the car and threw the bat down. I called Serena and told her to meet me at the motel in center city room 246.

Chapter 8

As Rell rolled down 17th street he bumped into Blaze and Onnie.
"Yo what up Rell? you know you just missed Crock?" Blaze inquired.
"Yeah I was busy. What he up to?"
"He just smashed Byron's head in with a bat." Blaze continued. "Yeah that nigga was fuckin with the product."
"Damn! That's what the fuck he get."
"He aight now he aint gotta worry about getting up on the wrong side of the bed anymore." Blaze said jokingly. Then said, "So what's up with you O.G.?"
"Aint shit, look "B" handle this for me." Rell asked tossing Blaze the keys to the

truck.

"I need twenty five for a drop too; I'll cover you out here."

"Aight." Blaze drove the truck around the block and took about fifteen minutes to get everything together then came back and gave Rell the keys back.

"A Rell can I roll with you cause my shifts over." Blaze asked.

"Nah lil nigga, it's just a switch. We can do something tonight probably."

"Aight be safe out there." Blaze said sincerely.

As Rell rolled off he cut the radio on, even though it was about a ten minute drive to 69th street. Once he got there he put his sixers' hat on and entered the station. The station was extremely crowded, to the point Rell was a bit noint about the drop. After walking around for about five minutes he posted up on a pay phone. He seen a Chicago bull's hat at a distance. But waited to see if he was rolling solo. He was walking towards Rell alone so Rell went to meet him. When Rell seen his face he immediately recognized him, but from where.

"What the situation?" "D" asked.

"Yo you look familiar." Rell said as he guided the man out.

"You do too but I can't pin point it" "D" replied.

"Lets get this business handled first. "Rell said "We can talk later when we aint hot." They walked to the Yukon and Rell asked,

"Is that the money?"

"Yeah eight hundred."

"Crock set everything up so I'll assume he knows you. But I still need to count it." Rell waited for a reaction but couldn't pick anything up.

"Don't worry about it, I can respect where you coming from." "D" handed Rell the bag and Rell counted out eight hundred G's.

"The truck is a gift." Rell said as he left, he disappeared in all the ruckus. Once he got back in the station he threw the hat in the trash and pulled out his cell and called Crock.

"Hello?"

"You aint busy are you?" Rell asked nervously

"Nah, I just finished eating. Why what's up?"

"I need you to pick me up at 69th street" Rell said

"Why something happen?" I asked as my voice escalated.

"Nah, Nah. I did that thing you asked me to do this morning."

"Oh, aight, I'll be there in about ten minutes. Be on the east side where the 55 runs."

"Aight."

Rell walked through the station and down to the platform where the 55 runs then he sat on the bench...

I finished washing my hands and left the bathroom. Back in the restaurant the waitress came over with my check.

$95.84 I gave her a $100 dollar bill and handed her a fifty.

"This for you baby girl."

"Thanks." she said with a smile. She looked attractive but I don't mess with people who are on shift. Although she looked like I made her day. As I was walking out the door, she came to the door and said,

"Thanks again."

"No problem Ma, maybe I'll see you again sometime?"

"I hope so." She said before getting back to her shift.

I got in the car and went to pick up Rell from 69th street. It was a nice day to be in the park. I pulled up and Rell jumped in throwing the bag in the back seat.

"Everything copastetic?" I asked pulling off.

"Yeah. Shit went smooth, he look familiar though."

"I know he went to school with us."

"Oh aight, a take me to the spot to drop this off then take me home."

"Aight, you got plans tonight?"

"Nah, why?"

"Cause stretch wanted to holla at me. Plus, I wanted to go to a club afterwards."

"I'll go. Oh Blaze wanted to go too."

"We'll pick him up too."

As we talked we rolled up to the spot on 17th street Rell handed Onnie the bag to put up then I took him home.

"So what club you wanna hit up?" Rell asked

"Shit we'll know when we find one."

"Oh aight." When we pulled up to his place my phone rang.

"I'll holla at you later tonight." Rell said getting out. I nodded and answered.

"Hello?"

"Where the fuck you at?" the voice spat

"Who the fuck is this calling me with fucking attitude?" I said returning fire.

"Serena! Nigga you told me to meet you here ten minutes ago."

"Damn my bad I had to pick my man up." I said heading to the motel.

"I'm like five minutes from you, you want me to grab some weed cause I got some Yac?"

"Just bring the Yac cause I'm smoking a blunt now." She said

"Aight"

I pulled into the parking lot between a suburban and a mustang. I grabbed the yac from the cooler and went into the motel. I took the elevator up to the second floor and knocked on the door.

"Come in." the voice said softly.

As I went into the room you could see the kitchen area. I walked around to the bedroom and Serena was lying in the bed with red lingerie on. I opened the cognac and took a long swig.

"Come over here and let me help you with that." She cooed. She was on her hands and knees, when she started to unbutton my jeans and pulled them down. It didn't take long for my boxers to follow suit. As she grabbed my dick she drank some yac, then stuffed it in her mouth. The warmth alone almost set me off early, but the yac had me elsewhere. I stopped her and pulled her off then stepped outta my jeans and boxers. I laid her on her back and slipped a condom on. She scratched at my chest but I caught her hands. Don't want any evidence of what I'm about to do left visible. When I slid in she was nice and wet. The first stroke she moaned. Then I picked up the pace to the verge of a wild man, yet she kept throwing that pussy back. I got tired of missionary so I grabbed and flipped her over. I started to stroke that pussy from the back and she started to yell.

"That's what the fuck I'm talking about, take this pussy! Make that shit yours!!"

I continued to pump away trying to shred this bitches insides, but she kept cheering and cussing the whole time.

"Damn, I'm about to cum." I yelled.

She jumped around and snatched off the condom then she inhaled my dick like a blunt, I in turn nutted in her mouth for the second time.

"Damn. I aint know a nigga had a stroke like that." She said as she wiped her mouth with the sheet. I looked at her and said,

"You got a good fucking shot Ma!" as I sprawled out on the bed exhausted.

"You better call me soon!" she said as she was getting dressed. I watched as she walked out. She was walking funny as hell, I started to laugh. She looked at me before she left. Soon after I jumped in the shower...

Chapter 9

Rell walked in to find an empty house. So he flopped in front of the T.V. and turned on Madden. About a good twenty minutes go by and in walked Mel with her hair all displaced and her shirt torn at the neck. Concerned Rell snapped.
"What the fuck! Yo what happened to you?"
"I was in a fight with some girl on Broad street." She replied.
"Are you aight?"
"Huh, you should see her."
"There wasn't no cop out there was it?"
"Nah, some old friends broke it up." she said as she begun to remove her coat and shoes.
"You know who she was?" Rell continued to ask questions.
"No! I didn't know her." She started to cry and ran into the bedroom.
Rell got up and paused the game and followed her back. She was taking her clothes off and Rell said,
"I just wanna make sure you aight. You my heart, at times I know I'm out there. But look at what I do. Sometimes I need to

be out there for us to survive." He pleaded his case.

"I know that I just want you to settle down with me." She said heading to the shower as Rell followed.

"Look boo, if I settle any more than I have then I'd be married!"

Before she stepped into the shower she looked at Rell and she smiled, then threw the towel at him. Rell went back into the living room and continued playing his game. It was about eight o'clock when Rell called Crocks crib and got the machine, then called his cell.

"Hello?"

"Yo what's the deal? You busy?" Rell asked.

"I'm on my way to the house to get in the shower again."

"So what time we all gonna roll?"

"Probably around ten, ten thirty." I said

"Aight, I'ma call Blaze and tell him and Onnie to come over."

"Aight holla at me at nine thirty."

"Bet!"

I pulled up to my place and the cell rang again.

"Damn hello."

"What's wrong baby?" Meme asked

"I just tripped what's up Ma?"

"Don't be Maing me I aint none of them ho's you be talking to on the streets." She said.

"Whoa, what's that all about?" I asked confused.

"You get on my nerves with that shit!"

"I'm sorry boo." I said sincerely.

As I got in the crib I got ready for the shower.

"Can me and the girls go out tonight?" she asked sounding nervous.

"Who all going with you?"

"Me, Melanie, Tabitha and Kim."

"Aight, I thought you were going to take freak ass Kelly."

"Nah, she don't know when to shut up."

"Aight love, call me later cause I gotta get a shower."

When I hung up I decided to take a long bath. When I got out I felt more energized. It was about ten minutes after nine, so I got dressed and turned on the PS2 and played online. After winning two games my phone rang.

"Yo"

"It's a quarter to ten, you coming?" Rell asked.

"Yeah, I'm coming now."

I hung up and cut the game and computer off, then grabbed my keys and left to Rells crib. It was only a five minute drive to his house. When I got there his door was open. I walked in and it was packed, Blaze, Onnie, Smooth and Rell were all playing Madden. It was tense in there with like eight hundred on the table. They were playing two on two, Blaze was playing with his younger brother smooth. He usually rolls with us when his brother isn't working. It looked like Rell was content with the game, Onnie was frustrated. The score was 35-28 in favor of the brothers.

"Yo, what's up Crock?" everyone spat at once.

"Aint shit I see yall found something to do."

"We about to cause an upset." Four minutes left Onnie and Rell are bringing the ball down the field.

"We gonna take they money, yeah we gonna stop them here and run the clock out."

"Shit I can't tell" Onnie said as he completed a pass across the middle for a first down at the thirty yard line.

"Aight, finish up cause I wanna set up a tournament. Five hundred a game or person. Single game elimination. Winner takes all." Everyone agrees in unison. I like playing tournaments cause I win a lot of them. I called for some pizzas and sodas, then I called stretch.

"Hello?" he answered.

"Yo what's the deal?"

"I'm hanging in there where you at?" he asked.

"Look I wont be able to make our little meeting tonight. I'm entertaining some guests, if you can feel where I'm coming from."

"Okay. Will I see you tomorrow?" he asked sternly.

"Why? What you got to tell me that's so important?" I asked becoming agitated

cause I know all he wanna do is talk.
"I'll tell you tomorrow" he responded.
"Aight" I hung up and went to see who
won the game.
"Yeah mother fucka-game time!" Rell said
jumping up grabbing the money.
"Damn, Blaze you blown your coverage."
"A crock who go first?" Onnie asked
"We gonna pick numbers out of a hat 1-5.
Top two play first and winner stays on.
Five hundred buys you a $2500 dollar pot
size, winner takes all."
        Onnie played smooth and smooth
controlled the whole game and won 42-28.
Rell was next to play smooth and Rell
managed to score on the kickoff, but this
game was tight all the way through. In
overtime Rell ran another kickoff back to
win 17-10. Blaze was up to play Rell, this
was damn near an identical game but Rell
kicked a 46 yard field goal to win the game
in the fourth quarter. I played Rell and
managed to come back in the fourth to
pull off the up set with a 24-21 win over
Rell.
"Damn, Rell went that far to sell out and
choke." I laughed and pocketed the
money...

Chapter 10

        As we finished we headed to our
cars. Blaze drove a 2000 Pathfinder. Onnie
rolled in a 2001 Eclipse and smooth was
riding in a 98 Celica. With half the team

together we headed to Jersey. On the way
we were flying. I drove but they were
racing. Smooth and Onnie were ballin out,
I couldn't believe how fast he had that car
going. When we pulled up in Jersey we
snapped back to our senses and went to a
club called Eutopia there were like ten
bitches going in, which helped our
decisions. The club appeared to be
jumping, there were chicks dancing on
stages the bar was full and to top it off
there was an oxygen bar. There was a lot
of white mother fuckas of or from some
clique in there too. Blaze went to the
chicks on the stages, Smooth stuck with
his brother. Onnie grabbed some drinks.
Me and Rell went looking for the owner,
the bartender who was also a female told
us he went upstairs for a moment. I
looked and seen a well dressed man
coming down so I went up to him.
"You fellas enjoying yourselves?" he asked.
"Look the names Crock and this my man
Rell." I said as we shook his hand. "Do you
by any chance have a V.I.P. lounge?"
"Of course, but who are you?! And how
will you pay for it?" he asked sizing us up.
"First of all, don't get sassy. Me and my
man just wanna be escorted to the V.I.P.
we got the money and we got respect, so
show us some. What's the price and take
us up." I said as I felt insulted.
"It's three grand a person and once a
member always a member. Everything's on
the house except the Don, Cris, and the

strippers."

I pulled out eight grand and Rell pulled out seven.

"You know who all came with us?"

"Yeah it was five of you. Damn is that fifteen grand?"

"Yeah, take us up!" Onnie came with the drinks.

"A Onnie tell Smooth and Blaze we're upstairs."

"Look let me apologize. My name is Travis and welcome to Eutopia."

As we went up a bunch of strippers came in as Travis was leaving. Two came and sat on both sides of me, Rell was getting a lap dance.

"Okay Rell I see you!" I said starting to feel the drinks in me so I laid back and chilled while the strippers continued to dance. Through all the music I could hear argument s, I looked down on the crowd and seen Smooth and some other nigga arguing. I couldn't see Blaze then Smooth pointed towards the back. I jumped up and called Rell and Onnie.

"Yo we got problems." as I ran past the dancers.

"What up?" Onnie asked as he ran behind me.

"Smooth about to have it out."

"Where Blaze?" Rell asked.

As we got to the back door I kicked it open and that's when the shots were fired. I pulled my hammer as I rolled outside. I looked up to see Onnie and Rell let off some shots of their own. Blaze was curled up by a dumpster with Smooth holding his head. "Rell call the ambulance!" I got up and went to Smooth. I was stricken but I couldn't show the pain in front of my mans.

"Yall see the car of the shooter?"

"Nah" Rell said on the phone.

"You fuckin right a blue Beamer with mirror tint. Aint to many with that mirror tint." Onnie said

"Smooth we gotta go, Rell call the ambulance!" I said as I tried to console the younger brother.

"They on the way Crock." Rell said.

"A Rell find that stripper you was with and pay her to drive Blaze's car home."

"Aight" he said running into the building.

I tried to help Smooth stand but you could tell he was hurt.

"No! leave me with him. He hissed at me.

"Then give me your guns so they don't detain you." He handed me two Beretta's. Feeling someone pull my shirt I looked. It was Onnie.

"Boss we gotta go."

"Here I come."

"Now!" he yelled. "The cops are on their way."

I stood and told Smooth to call me as soon as he can. The club was partially empty so we got through fairly easy. The owner was at the door, he looked to be signaling me over.

"What do you want I'm in kind of a hurry."

"I know who shot your friend. He's a member of a local gang called the diplomats.
"You know anything on there whereabouts?"
"No but most be at a bar called Forbidden Rhealm. It's about a five minute ride from here. The person he was arguing with goes by Razor." He finished then ran upstairs. As I left Rell and Onnie were already in their cars. There was a dancer in the Pathfinder. I got in my car and we all left towards Rells crib. While on the way I seen an ambulance racing past us. I called Rell on the cell.
"Yo"
"A Rell I know who was arguing with Blaze and Smooth."
"Who was he?"
"Some nigga called Razor who rep the diplomats. I was told by the club owner."
"You believe him?"
"I don't know but we can find out."
"How?" Rell asked.
"He said they mostly be at a bar called Forbidden Rhealm."
"Lets hit that shit now." He said angrily.
"Nah we gotta plan this shit out first. We gotta play the cards right cause that's their domain. They could be waiting for us too."
"So what the fuck we gonna do? Sit around and wait for them to slip up?"
"Nah, we gonna put a watcher in the bar and slide the owner some change to have

him or her bartend or something. He or she can find out who Razor is and the times they show up and how many show up."

"I feel you. Yo I'ma tell Onnie, so holla at me in the morning cause I'm going home.

"Aight."

I pulled up next to the Pathfinder and pointed to my phone as I was calling the car phone in the Pathfinder.

"Hello?" she answered.

"Listen Ma my man is going home so follow me, I'ma take you to where the truck go and then I'll drive you home."

"Okay!"

I turned onto Blazes block and pulled up in front of his crib. She parked and got out, she got in the car and handed me the keys.

"So where you live at Ma?"

"You really don't have to take me home you can drop me at the bus station." She said sincerely.

"Ma its three thirty and the buses run by the hour and it's chilly out."

"I can manage."

"I would invite you to my crib but I do have a girl. I just don't want you to be out there alone."

"You're sweet but I've done it before."

I started towards Broad and Olney and parked out front on Broad.

"Listen, maybe we can talk until the bus comes, so you don't have to wait in the cold."

"Aight, what you wanna talk about?"
"How about nuclear physics and Genome therapy! Psyche Nah, I'm fucking with you." I said as I broke out laughing.
"You have a pretty smile." She said softly.
"I looked around me and out the back window.
"Who? You aint talking about me. Shit you must have had some drinks cause I don't get many compliments. Don't let no one know you said that, I try to keep my tough guy rep." I joked some more.
"You should get them. What your girl keeping you happy?"
　　　The buses started to come so I coped out.
"Oh here comes a bus." I handed her some money and she left saying I hope to see you back at the club soon! Maybe you can take me home next time, you know for our second date!" she laughed and closed the door.
"It's been a long fueling day." I said to myself as I headed home, still thinking about shorty I don't even know her name...

Chapter 11

As the ambulance came it looked like a movie. They came racing out of it with their blue uniforms and big black bags.
"Sir, you must give us room. What happened?" the female asked as she put some shit on Blazes' arm to test his blood pressure.

"He was shot!" Smooth said nervously.

They continued asking questions as he just watched distraught as Blaze laid in his distant state. They put him on a gurney and rolled him into the ambulance. Smooth ran to his car to follow them as they raced off. He still couldn't believe Blaze let it go down like that, all he had to do was stop. That bitch wasn't worth four bullets. Now he might not survive the night.

"How was he supposed to know it was a set up?" Smooth yelled to himself.

"I couldn't even see it coming!" he finished. Damn a red light, I aint fen to run a red light with that suka ass cop over there. He watched as the ambulance sped off and turned right. He said fuck it and turned right and looked down every left turn to see if he could find the ER. As he came up on another light he seen it and turned down the street. Once in the parking lot he parked and ran in after them. The place was booming with people, shit was crazy. Patients were walking around in walkers and I.V.'s in their arms. People were in wheel chairs with bags of piss under them. Nurses were helping some people with their medicine. Smooth did his best to keep up with the paramedics and doctors. They ran into a room that had O.R. #2 on the top of the door. Smooth ran in and was interrupted by a nurse.

"Sir, excuse me sir! You can't be in here now. The doctor has to work and he can't

do that with you contaminating the room."
She said as she was pushing him towards
the door.
"Yo fuck that he's my brother!" Smooth
snapped.
"I understand sir. But you can't help by
being in the way. Let us do our job, and
we'll do our best trust me!" she said as she
tried to console him.
"Aight, get the fuck off me!"
        he stood outside the O.R. and
watched them work. Ten minutes passed
and the doctor came out.
"Are you the patient's family member?"
"Yeah, how is he doc?" Smooth asked.
"we were able to stabilize him but he
seems to be in a coma due to post
traumatic stress."
"Hold up man I don't know what the hell
you just said!" he said confused.
"He's in a deep sleep from being shot and
losin so much blood. There is another
thing!" the doctor said and paused to sign
a clip board.
"What!"
"One of the bullets nicked his spine there
is no way we can tell if he has any
movement in his lower extremities. We
have to wait till he comes to, in order to
remove the bullet. That's the safest way."
"Damn, so he cool huh?"
"Yes he's okay for now, he wont feel any
pain." The doctor replied.
"Thanks doc for everything."
        Smooth walked to the waiting room

and sat in the back. It was about six o'clock and he was tired. He wound up falling asleep in the waiting room...

As I woke up Meme was still sleeping. I walked to the bathroom and found a plethora of bodies on the floor. Tabitha and Kim were sleeping on the floor by the bedroom door. Melanie was stretched out on my couch. I got in the bathroom and took a piss, when I was done I flushed and dropped the seat. I washed my hands and looked into the mirror and started thinking. I can holla at Stretch or Stan for a bartender or table busser . I washed my face and started to brush my teeth. Rell probably sleep, damn I gotta find someone to replace Blaze. I got a lot of shit to tend to today. I crawled in the bed and whispered in Memes ear.

"Boo, you up?"

"Hum." She moaned.

"None of your friends gotta go to work do they?"

"Hum-um." She mumbled trying to say no.

"I gotta go check on Blaze, he was shot yesterday." Her eyes opened and focused on me.

"How bad was it?" she asked looking concerned,

"I don't know Smooth hasn't called me."

"Can I come with you?"

"Boo I need you here to watch the house you know I don't trust them."

"Okay be careful out there!"

"Aight."

I kissed her on her forehead and made my way through the maze of bodies to the door. I grabbed my keys and locked up behind me. I remote started my car and put the best of Big and Pac on. I drove to the spot on 17th street and found Onnie and Buck hard at work. Although Buck is one of my door men he still picked up the slack until word comes back on Blaze.

"Boss." Onnie called, "any word on Blaze?"

"Nah I'm going to check on him today. Have you seen Rell?"

"Nah."

"Call me if you do."

"Aight"

"Uh Buck? Good lookin on covering for "B"."

"It aint about nothing" Buck said you took care of me, I take care of you."

I left to holla at Stan down at the lounge, when I got there the phone was still not answered by Smooth, as I tried to call. I walked in and the place was busy. I went up to the bar and called Stan over.

"What's up? Can't you see we're busy?"

"Yo Blaze was shot yesterday!"

"Damn how is he?" he looked concerned. I'm not sure yet I'ma see him after I leave. I need a favor though. The nigga who shot him be at some bar in Jersey called the Forbidden Rhealm."

"What could I do to help?"

"I need a bartender or busser who's loyal to put in there to be my eyes and ears."

"Why?"

"Cause we need to find out how often they be in there and how many they roll with."
"I could ask Miranda she's an excellent bartender and she's been with me for six years."
"Aight ask her I'll go set everything up with the bar owner"
"Aight"

I left the bar heading to the gas station. After I filled the tanks I went to Jersey. I rode to the P3 to holla at stretch. "Crock!" Said a familiar voice. So I turned and looked to see stretch coming at me.
"A Crock, I thought you wouldn't make it."
"Yeah, A you know who owns the Forbidden Rhealm?" I asked.
"Of course. Why?"
"My friend is looking for work, maybe you could put in a good word for her.
"She's a good bartender."
"Aight, what's her name?"
"Miranda!"
"Oh I wanted to thank you yesterday!"
"For what." I asked confused "I did something for you?"
"Right keep it quiet. Remember that little problem I had?"
"Oh I didn't…" he cut me off saying "Don't worry my lips are sealed!"

Shit that's what the fuck I'm afraid of nigga can't shut the fuck up. He continued with.
"They were three head members of a gang called the diplomats. Word is they nervous cause they don't know who hit them. It's

about six more members in their team, and one of them shot someone yesterday."
"Damn that's deep. Oh will you be able to handle that for me? Oh and don't worry about that other thing!"
"Yeah I got you. If you ever need anything ask me."
"Aight..."

Splash... water smacks Rell in the face. He tried to stand but couldn't due to his hands being tied to a chair. His eyes are open but all he can see is black. Panic started to set in.
"What the fuck is this shit?" he yelled but was met with a swift body shot. That knocked him over in the chair. He felt himself being picked back up.
"We will be asking all the questions!" the voice spat.
"You knew my brother Linx didn't you?"
"What! I don't know who your talking about." Rell said before a jab closed his mouth. Rell couldn't think straight, but the rusty taste in his mouth told him the end was near.
"Nigga don't lie you in no position to play hard ball. Now word on the street is you shot my brother and cousin." Rell could hear steps moving back and forth.
"I shot a lot of people." Rell said.
"So you think you smart huh?" maybe this will help you remember." The voice snickered. In the darkness Rell heard the hammer cock.
"So you don't remember?"

BOOM! A shot rang out and Rell could feel the pain in his left foot race up through the rest of his body.

"Aah! What the fuck. I told you I shot a lot of mother fuckas. I don't know your brother!" Rell pleaded his best under the circumstances.

"So my sources aint reliable?" the voice asked.

"Look I don't know who the fuck you talking about. Who ever it is they got it fucked up!" Rell hissed from the pain.

"Nah, Nah, Nah! I think you know him. He go by Dex!"

"That's bullshit Dex is dead! He aint tell you shit." In the distance Rell heard a familiar ring, it was his cell phone. He couldn't pin point where it was, he knew it was his though. Then he heard whispers.

"Find that phone and bring it to me!" the voice spat

Rell knew it was at least three niggas in the room with him. He tried to loosen the bonds on the chair to no avail.

"I got all day mother fucka how much blood you got left in your tank?"

BOOM!! Another shot rang out and he felt another sharp pain pierce through his body. When he realized he was hit in his knee he was hit with another body shot.

"Mother fucka, I don't know what you looking for so you might as well kill me." There was another ring and after a couple rings he heard a familiar voice.

"Yo!! I'm either out or sleep so leave a message and I'll get back. Beep!!"

He started to feel light headed as his legs were going numb. The voice spoke still unfamiliar.

"I want to know who killed my brother, and I think you know who did it."

Man look I know I'm dead either way so yeah, I know who killed your brother!" Rell said as he fought through the pain.

"Who? Tell me and I may spare your life."

Rell thought for a while and said

"One of them niggas from the diplomats killed him. I figure I'm dead anyway so how he gonna kill me again?" he said laughing to himself at his sinister plan.

"Yeah"

The room seemed restless and there seemed to be an argument, Rell yelled to be heard.

"That's right, that niggas name is Razor, he killed your brother and told me if I say anything I'd be next."

"Nah, this nigga lying man."

Rell was met with another body shot then one to the jaw.

"Yo, I aint kill Linx or Boo man, he talking about I killed his cousin."

"What nigga?" another voice spat. Rell heard that voice before but from where?

"I said I aint kill his cousin." The voice said again.

"Oh, yeah I thought you said that!" the familiar voice said. Rell heard a hammer cock.

"He said his brother not cousin you snake mother fucka!"

Then he heard ten shots ring out, then it was a sense of calm.

"Yo! I aint seen shit you can let me go."

"You right I can but I still don't believe you. I'ma stop all this bullshit right now!"

the cloth was ripped from his head and when his eyes focused they saw what was the barrel of a pump. All he could say was,

"Shit!"

BOOM! He felt his body get thrown back in to the chair, his body started shaking and he saw a light get brighter.

Then he heard his name.

"Rell! Rell! Rell!"

"Aaaaah!" Rell yelled and woke up to see Melanie standing over him, still shaking him.

"Damn you were having a nightmare." She said.

"You was screaming about some diplomats and some nigga getting shot."

"Damn a nigga going through it."

Rell got out of bed and took a long ass shower...

Chapter 12

The block was still pumpin so buck went in to re-up. Onnie was eyeing this funny dressed nigga for a minute, so he stopped his business and he stashed his product around the bend. Buck came back out and seen him, he played like he never seen him. Dude came up to Onnie and asked,

"You got any of that good get high?" Onnie looked at him like he was stupid.

"Yeah the shit that'll get you high up out of my face."

"You aight?" Buck asked from a distance.

"Nah! The leaves are falling." Onnie spat meaning something's up. Buck stopped what he was doing and walked around the bend. We all pretty much grew up in the neighborhood so we know the ins and outs if we need to skate. Onnie looked at this nigga and seen something on his shirt and it wasn't a label.

"This nigga!" he said to himself. "Yo, you wearing a wire?" he spat. The fiend seemed to have lost the pain in his back, cause now he was standing up straight.

"What you talking bout man?" as dude spoke his voice changed slightly.

"What the fuck!" Onnie thought "It's official this nigga a cop." He continued to think to himself then he said.

"Damn, they let that dog out again." The man turned and looked. When he turned back his jaw was met with one of Onnie's left hooks. The man fell flat on his ass. Onnie broke and cut straight into an alley. He hopped a few fences and climbed a few gates. He thought he was safe then felt a sting in the back of his head then seen a flash of light. He turned to run but his legs didn't seem to respond. He felt light headed and fell to the ground...

Smooth was up and walking around in the hospital in search of the kitchen or a vending machine. Finally a vending machine with some cakes and shit. He inserted his money and pressed a button. Then the door to the machine opened. He wound up eating a blueberry donut for breakfast with an orange juice. Once he finished he walked back to the desk.

"Did they move my brother? He wasn't in the O.R."

"Yeah they moved him to room 304." Said the receptionist.

"Thanks."

Smooth went to be by his brothers' side. But when he got there a doctor was coming out and said.

"You're the brother correct?"

"Yeah."

"Sorry to say but there's been little improvement."

"Damn."

He went in and sat by the bed. He took a look at his cell phone; ten missed calls and three new messages. He listened to the first message.

"Yo Smooth, its Crock, I was calling to see how things are going with you and Blaze. Call me when you find something out. I'll be up to see yall tomorrow. Holla at me later..."

The second message said,

"Stevie where are you? You too good to call

your mother and that brother of yours.
When you have time call me..."
    The final message said,
"So that's it? You don't call me anymore.
What, you done with me now? I aint done
nothing to you for you to just be igging me
like this. That's fucked up..."
    Damn he said I forgot to pick her up
now she acting crazy. He decided to call
his girl.
"Hello?" she answered.
"It's me I just got your message." Smooth
said
"What you want?!" she said snapping back
at him.
"Look calm down."
"What you talking about calm down? I'm
tired of you standing me up. See that's
what's wrong with you young ass niggas."
Knowing she's three years his senior.
"Shut the fuck up! I'm tired of you talking
shit. You so fuckin selfish, it's always
about you. Well if you would let me talk
you would have known my brother wa..."
as she cut him off he felt his temper start
to rise.
"Your brother that's all you talk about,
what yall a couple now?" she said.
"I swear I'ma get you fucked up. If you'd
stop bitchin you would know my brother
was shot yesterday. That's why I couldn't
pick you up. I'm at the fuckin hospital."
Smooth snapped.
"Oh my God, I'm so sorry. I didn't know
how he is doing?" she asked sounding

apologetic.

"He's in a fuckin coma!" he yelled still agitated. "You know what I can't talk to you right now." He hung up and called his mother.

"Hello?"

"Mom?" Smooth said

"Stevie is that you?"

"Yeah mom, I haven't called you cause Bennie was shot yesterday and he's in a coma right now."

"Oh my baby was shot! Where are yall at?" she asked.

"Jersey county hospital."

"I'm coming don't you go anywhere!"

"Aight mom," Smooth put his coat over him and laid back in his chair...

As I left the P3 I rolled to the hospital to check on my lil nigga. I pulled up in the parking lot and grabbed my keys then went in the hospital. I went to the receptionist to ask for the room of a Turner.

"Turner huh? Well let me see. Here we are he's in room 304."

"Thanks." I went in the room planning to be here a little bit. I walked in to see Smooth and his mom.

"Hi Mrs. Turner."

I gave her a hug and apologized for not being able to do more for him.

"Don't worry about it David if you were with them you could be in the same situation. Thanks for coming." She said.

"You know you like a mother to me so I

had to check up on the family."

"That's sweet of you baby."

"Tenisha told me to give you a kiss for her."

I leaned in and gave her a kiss on the cheek.

"She apologizes for not being able to make it." I finished telling her.

"Thanks she's a sweet girl. When yall going to have some babies?" she asked.

"My baby Stevie always fighting with Tameka. I don't expect any grand kids from those two!"

"Mrs. Turner I don't think she's into me that much." I said trying to be modest.

"I don't think so." She replied "Yall got that chemistry." As she laughed.

"Yeah" Smooth said in agreement. "Yall can't be separated. Not like me and meka we can't stay together."

"Hold up yall not gonna team up on me about life with me and Tenisha! I came to show my respect and pray for Blaze."

I put a card in the window and went to Smooth and whispered.

"This for you and your moms," And handed him $1500 dollars and made sure Mrs. Turner couldn't see the exchange.

"Holla at me if you need anything."

"Thanks Crock!"

I left the hospital to holla at Miranda at the lounge...

Chapter 13

Feeling groggy Onnie woke up in a room with two chairs and a table. He looked around to find he was alone. There was a camera in the north corner of the room above the door, there also was a red light blinking on it. He figured he was being taped right now. There was a trickle of something running down his cheek. He couldn't tell what it was due to the hand cuffs behind his back. The door opened and in walked two detectives. One was an old fat mother fucka with a bad Toupee. The other looked familiar to him. He was the one he ran from. He stood at about six feet and had a slender build. His name tag said Det. A. Sterling.

"Aah! Mr. Oliver, we meet again." Said Sterling.

"Man fuck you!" Onnie spat.

"Oh such hostility. We don't want anything but cooperation." The fat man said.

"And who the fuck are you?" Onnie snapped.

"My name is detective McKnight. Sam McKnight" the door was still open but the fat detective was standing there.

"I don't know shit so I know this won't be long. So don't be fucking with me all day."

"I seen you making sales today!" Sterling said.

"You aint seen me do shit, you aint find me with shit so get the fuck on with it!"

the fat detective sat in front of Onnie and lit a cigarette. He offered one to Onnie who shook his head Nah. Detective McKnight snapped his fingers and was handed a manila folder from Sterling. Sterling went and closed the door. McKnight opened the folder and it had a lot of papers in it, but what caught Onnie's attention was the two photographs of Boo. One was a picture of Boo outlined in yellow chalk. The second was one of his head viewing a massive hole with dried blood and tissue hanging from it.

"You know who this is?" he asked showing Onnie the pictures.

"Nah, was it someone of importance? Cause you wasting my time with this dumb shit." Onnie said.

"His name is or was Brandon Collier and he was 23 years old, before his brains were forced from his skull.

"Sounds painful." Onnie said sarcastically.

"Shut up! You shut your fucking mouth you piece of shit." Sterling snapped and walked over to his chair.

"What am I suppose to be scared? Look get my lawyer in here and we ca..."he was cut off by a punch that made him bite down on his tongue. The blood started to flow in his mouth.

"I told you to shut your cock sucker!" Sterling said laughing. Onnie spit blood from his mouth and said,

"You pork eatin pussies aint getting shit outta me!" and continued with, "I told you

I don't know this dude. He may have deserved it for all I care." Det. Sterling kept pacing back and forth behind him when Det. McKnight flipped through the folders and some more pictures were on the top of the stack. These pictures were of Linx, one was of his chalked out line, and the other showed the graphic content of his body riddled with bullets . one section of his chest had a hole so big you could fit a fist through it. His stomach had at least ten or fifteen holes in it.

"I suppose you don't know him either huh?" the detective asked.

"Nah, but I'd rather go out like Brandon with one shot, instead of being a tribute to a horror flick." Onnie said continuing his sarcasm.

The fat detective looked frustrated and then he stood.

"My patients are growing thin with you Mr. Oliver we already know you and these two victims had past squabbles."

"That don't mean I killed them, they had beef with a lot of people on the streets. They just victims of what some call circumstances."

"So you know nothing about their murders?"

"Fuck no!"

"Where were you on the night of the 16th at four o'clock?"

"with my girl. You know, I do like to please my woman. Something yall need to worry more about than fuckin with me about two dead niggas! Yall probably killed them with yall slimy asses."

Onnie felt a blow coming so he steadied himself and the door opened. There stood a woman in plain clothes holding a couple of folders.

"I know you were not about to assault that defenseless prisoner?!"

"Yeah hit me now Sterling! Your boss show up and you get soft."

"What are the charges?" she asked.

"We haven't charged him with anything. He was free to leave at his will." McKnight said.

"Free to leave! How can I leave with these hand cuffs on. I asked for my lawyer and only got a busted lip."

"You have this man detained against his will and you denied him his lawyer? Remove the cuffs and meet me in my office pronto!" the woman spat.

Detective Sterling took the cuffs off and told me to get out of his face. As Onnie was leaving he said,

"Yeah pussy steal me now, I'll fuck your bitch ass up! You gonna get yours Sterling, Seriously!" Onnie left. When he got outside he called Buck.

"Hello?"

"Yo these niggas tried to pin two homicides on me."

"For real? How you get out?" Buck asked.

"some bitch came when that nigga was fuckin me up and told them to let me go."

"You aint have nothing on you did you?"

"Nah, I was clean."
"Aight you coming back or you gonna lay back for the day?"
"I'ma fall back until tomorrow. I might still be hot. I'ma pick up my money cause I gotta call Crock to pay him today." Onnie finished
"Aight, holla if anything comes up!"
"Aight..."

Chapter 14

Rell left the club and went to the Gallery. He picked up a couple pair of Roc-a-wear jeans and two pair of sneakers. When he found a florist he walked up and was greeted.
"Hello how are you today?" the woman asked.
"I'm good thanks for asking."
"My name is Amber, is there anything in particular I can help you with?"
"Yes I need flowers sent to 1846 price 19138 for a Mrs. Turner."
"Okay would you like a dozen or half dozen?"
"You could send a dozen."
"And would you like red roses or white roses?"
"Mix it up for me."
"Okay that'll be a total of $34.95 what would you like on the card?"
"Um sorry I couldn't be there with you in this time of need. I send all my love with

these flowers. From Terrell." He handed her forty dollars and began to think, maybe it'll be nice to send Mel something for a change.

"Excuse me do you have any packages that are sent same day delivery?"

"Yes would you like to put one together?" she asked nicely.

"Could you put a dozen red roses in with a box of chocolates and a Teddy bear?" Rell asked with a bit of excitement.

"And what would you like on the card?"

"I know I haven't been the best of boyfriends, but I love you more for sticking with me. Love Rell."

"Okay the package will be $43.89." Amber continued. "Would you like it wrapped and tied with a bow?"

"Yeah that'll be nice thanks." Rell gave her a fifty and asked her, to keep the change.

"Thank you sir."

Rell left and headed towards the pizza stop and bumps into his man Mil who use to sling and rob with him. They got separated when Rell got booked. Mil is a little like Dex but with a nastier way of handling niggas. Yo the kid is sick!

"Yo, what's the fuckin deal?" Rell asked as he offered a dap to his man.

"The same old shit!" Mil gave dap and a hug to his man.

"Yo it's been a minute dog, what you been up to?" Rell asked.

"When you got clipped I went on a little spree. You know get down or lay down!" he said with a smile.

"I feel you . Look we always looking for handlers or a nigga that moves out, you feel me?"

"Aight, but if I come my man Streetz gotta come. I only work for profit, same as Streetz."

"Look Crock running shit, he may put yall on a contact. He love niggas who move out. I can put a word in for yall if you want?" Rell explained.

"You handle that and I'ma let Streetz know what's going down."

"Aight." Rell said pulling out some paper and writing something on it.

"Look I gotta go but here's my handle get at me." He finished writing and handed him his handle.

"Oh a Mil you know Blaze just got popped so Crock may plug yall in with us cause we about to wax some niggas."

"Solid! Tell us where and when and we'll be there." Mil said with his patented smirk.

"Before I go where those bitches at? They usually swarming behind you like flies on shit."

"You know me I stick to the mix, I never be seen with one chick. If I aint got more than one , I wont have none."

"Ha! Ha! Ha! You still a funny nigga, I'll see you!" Rell said giving dap and rolled out. When he walked up to the pizza shop he grabbed a slice of plain pizza and went to the car. When he got to the trunk he put his jeans and sneakers in and as he pulled from the Gallery he stopped at a store in China town to pick up some General Tso chicken and a thing of lemonade. Afterwards Rell was on his way home to put his shit up and then he was gonna go check on Blaze. His phone rang.

"Yo what's the deal?" he answered.

"Yo I'm on my way to holla at Stan. You went to holla at Smooth and Mrs. Turner yet?" I asked.

"Nah, I was going to drop my shit off then holla at them."

"Tonight we need everyone together cause we gotta strategize."

"Aight, oh I just bumped into my man Mil at the Gallery. Him and his peoples are cut throat ass niggas. I told them you may want them for couple jobs." Rell said busting their reps.

"I'll see them when the time is with us..."

I was about five minutes from the lounge and decided to grab a cheese steak from Ed's pizza house. I also grabbed some cheese fries and a large Pepsi. I waited until I reached the lounge to eat in my booth. The bar wasn't that busy but there was still enough to be a satisfactory kind of day. I went in towards my usual booth and Stan said,

"Yo Crock, you heading back?"

"Yeah is Miranda here?"

"She over there, I'll send her back to you. Oh she said she'll help you out too."

"Aight"

After about five minutes she came back. She was about 5'4" and thick as hell, I mean shorty was tight. She had a hooters T-shirt that showed off her stomach. She had some tight jeans that rode low around the hips and back, and she had a navel ring. She was rockin some tight braids and when she sat down that's when I noticed she had green eyes. That's what took the cake.

"Hey Crock. Stan told me you were looking for a bartender to be your eyes and ears." She said with a little of an accent.

"Damn, Ma you lookin real sharp, you got green eyes too. I don't know, I may not wanna put you in that situation. You look more like wifey material!" giving my compliments.

"Come on Crock don't do that shit! I really need the money. I promise I'll be careful, I'll give you all the information at the end of my shifts. I'll stay out of their way and I'll be friendly." She pleaded.

"Don't mind me asking but why would you put yourself in harms way just for a little extra money?" I asked.

"It's better than selling my ass on the corner. Plus I have another mouth to feed."

"Damn what's up with the baby's father?"

"That nigga turned out to be a lame, but I'm over him."

"Look I don't want you to get hurt Ma." I said.

It looked like her eyes glazed over then she

put her hand on my thigh. I guess for incentive.

"Please give me a chance, I'll be safe." she began to beg.

"I'll see how things go the first week, but you know you may see people get shot and killed. The cops may ask you questions and threaten you about taking your child."

"I aint gonna move on anyone plus I'll be workin."

"Aight Ma you convinced me." I pulled out two hundred and gave it to her. "This your first payment. I spoke with my man so all we have to do is get you started."

I was finished and she got up and cleaned the table. She turned around and her ass was like Damn!! I had to ask. "Miranda?" she turned to look at me. "Do you have a man holdin you down?"

"No! all the men I meet are ass holes and selfish." She turned and walked to the bar and looked at me once more. I smiled and finished my Pepsi...

Chapter 15

As Mil and Streetz were moving through the Gallery they were discussing the opportunity that was laid in front of them. Streetz, who was known for clippin niggas at dice games. There's no way to stop him when he starts bussing except for him empting his clip. Mil, who is unpredictable, he'll aim and shoot and hope the money doesn't get bloody. Then

there's times where he'll trunk a mother
fucka and use all types of methods to
make them scream. As they pull out some
chairs at a pizza shop Mil said,
"Look we can make some easy money by
just doing what we do!"
"I only heard of these niggas, I don't know
what they really hittin for." Streetz said.
"I know them we tight we just aint been
rolling together cause they got booked like
six months ago. They big paper makers
and we have a chance to get in with their
clique." Mil pleaded his case.
"But we aint broke so why look for more
money? the bigger the money the bigger
the risk we gotta take." Streetz spat
"Look you my man, I respect what you
have to say, but we can try to stay afloat
by robbing some penny pushers or we can
get with their team and take out some
heavy hitters. We might be able to take
over a couple strips." Mil said with his
smirk.
Streetz finished his piece of pizza and
said,
"I don't know but you said they thorough
then I'm with you fuck it..."
        ...Back at the hospital there seemed
to be very little to no change in Blazes
condition. Smooth was doing his best to
console his mother. She fell asleep about
an hour ago, he put his coat on her to
keep her warm. Smooth found another
nurse in the hallway and asked for an
additional blanket. She eventually brought

one to him about ten minutes later. Smooth took the opportunity with his mother being sleep to go grab some hot cocoa from the cocoa machine in the lobby. When he returned to the room he called Tameka.

"Hello?" she answered.

"Hey baby girl how are you?" Smooth asked.

"I'm chillin, thinking about you. I've also been waiting for you to come home."

"I'll be there within an hour cause I gotta take a shower. I'll just come over there and take it there."

"Baby I'm sorry for snapping earlier, and I'm sorry about your brother." She spoke sincerely.

"Meka don't worry about it I'll be home soon." Smooth said as he was leaving the building.

"Aight I love you!" she said.

"I hope so, love you!"

Once he got in his car he drove straight home which was about a thirty five to forty minute drive. He was in no mood to be driving fast so he rode the limit all the way home. Once he got there the house smelled sweet like lavender or something. Smooth wanted to jump in the shower but the smell was intoxicating. Tameka waltzes in the living room with some red high heel pumps and a red negligee.

"You look sexy as hell. I'ma jump in the shower real quick, cause I was out for a couple of days."

"I aint going anywhere so take your time. I just wanna apologize the best way I know how!" she said speaking seductively.

Smooth was enticed by her notions and headed for the shower. As he was lathering up he couldn't stop thinking how of she was trying to keep him happy, he decided it was his turn to do the pleasing. He rinsed off and got out of the shower. Once he got out of the shower he slipped his boxers and socks on. He went into the bed room and there laid Meka in the bed.

"I thought you were never coming out." She said

"Well didn't wanna keep you."

"You could never keep me too long."

Smooth climbed into the bed and crawled up to his woman. He kissed her then she attempted to lower herself to please her man.

"No! Baby let me do the honors."

He pulled her up and lowered himself and pulled her negligee off then began to give his woman some oral pleasure. An hour seemed to have passed and Meka couldn't fight the urges and began to moan and scream. She could feel her orgasm stirring up. Smooth felt her legs twitching and then she let rip as her legs clamped around his head. Smooth continued to stroke her clit with tongue and fingers. He waited until she was finished and then looked up. Her face looked crazy; she looked like she'd been relieved of enormous stress and tension. She pulled Smooth up and kissed him. "I love you baby, I do with all my heart." She said looking exhausted

"And I love you." Smooth replied.

"Will you stay true to me or do you still need time to vent yourself? Cause I wanna commit to you and only you." Meka said with such sincerity that a tear touched her eyes.

"I'd love to settle down with you but when Crock or Rell need me I'm there for them."

"They not your family, they aint your friends. All they want is more money and more power." She said angrily.

"That may be the case about the money and power but they are also respected. Plus they'll never let anything happen to me if they can stop it." Smooth said. Trying to reassure his girl.

"I know you gonna do what you want anyway. Just be careful!"

"I will."

They both rolled over and went to sleep...

Meme and Mel were busy in the Gallery. Meme bought a pair of Prada shoes and a matching bag. Mel bought a pair of air force ones with the yellow checks and a matching hand bag. They were walking around and they seen a store that sold hats and Jerseys. They went in and Meme knew what it was that she wanted. She bought a sixers fitted and a Iverson Jersey for Crock. The Jerseys were on sale buy two and get the third free. She

bought another A.I. Jersey that was a six XL and she got a McNabb Jersey that was a five XL. She told Mel.
" You should get one for you and Rell."
"Just grab him an Iverson Jersey and a McNabb Jersey. See I'm getting Crock an Iverson and McNabb Jersey."
"Yeah I'll do the same."
        They purchased their items and then went to the food court and ate and talked for a while...

Chapter 16

Ten minutes went by and Miranda came back to my booth.
"What time you wanna got to the bar?" she asked.
"We can go check it out when you finish your shift."
 "My shifts over in about ten minutes. I'll see if Stan will let me leave early cause we're not as busy." She said as she left I couldn't do much but adore the physique. I was ready to roll so I waited a couple minutes then called Onnie.
"Hello?" he answered.
"Yo you still working or you finished?"
"Nah, I fell back for the day."
"What! I hope it's a good fuckin reason you aint out there getting that money!" I said snapping.
"I was arrested today. There was some funny lookin nigga on the strip so I

stashed my shit."
"What they try to get you with?" I asked.
"They tried to pin two bodies on me, some niggas named Boo and Lynx."
"Damn you aight though?"
"Yeah I came straight home after I picked your money up."
"Look I'll get that shit later, I'm busy now."
"Aight"
I hung up and wondered how I would fix this if it became a problem. Onnie's a thorough nigga but I can't risk him turning over. I'ma have Buck watch him.
"You ready?" Miranda asked. Not knowing she came back.
"Oh yeah, my bad I was elsewhere."
I remote started the car as I was leaving the bar. I unlocked Miranda's door and walked around to get in. I threw some Pac "Better Dayz" in the disc changer. We drove to Jersey with very little to say to each other until we crossed the bridge. After we turned off she asked.
"So what's a man of your stature doing wrong, to not have a wife?" she asked without looking at me.
"Ma, I do a lot of things wrong, but there is a woman that has been down with me for a while now."
"And she hasn't faked a pregnancy or something foolish to try to trap you?"
"Damn you got your mind in the gutter. First of all we grew up together in the same hood. We been tight since we were babies. All the dumb shit is for suckas not

for us."

"Aight I was just asking don't hurt nothing." She said with a smile.

"Well don't! cause that's some slimy ass shit for a woman to do!"

We continued talking for a minute then arrived at the bar. The place looked clean from the outside and even nicer on the inside. I couldn't believe a mother fucka from this kind of spot would be in a gang. The bar had mirrors behind the drinks. The bartender was cleaning a cup with a white T-shirt and a pair of denim jeans. They had booths in the back with mirrors on the ceilings. They even had a stage with stools around it. I guess it's for Karaoke. The place was dead so me and Miranda went to the bartender.

"Sorry fellas the bar is closed until eleven o'clock."

"Don't worry about it we're here to see the owner." I said.

"Are you Crock?" he asked as he placed the cup on the shelf behind him.

"Yeah"

"We heard you were bringing someone to help me out."

"Here she is." I said as I stepped to the side.

"Hi, my name is Miranda." As she introduced herself.

"And I'm Michael. I'm pleased to have met you." He continued with, "I have to test your skills if you don't mind." I sat down and watched as they continued to work

wonders with their drinks.
"Is there anything else I need to do?" she
asked
"I'm afraid that's it."
"When could I start?" she asked.
"Today if you can."
"Aight, Crock thanks" she said as she gave
me a kiss that would have made some
think twice about us being friends.
"I have to do something so here's my
number, call me if you need anything."
        As I was leaving the bar my cell
rang.
"Hello?"
"What are you doing?" the voice was
familiar but I couldn't pinpoint from who I
knew it.
"You call and don't let anyone know who
you are!" I said
"Damn, we have an intimate connection
and you forget who it was with. That's
dangerous." The voice replied.
"Yo who the fuck is this?" becoming more
frustrated.
"Stop playing."
"I aint got time for games." Then I hung
the phone up. I was in the car and decided
to go home and take a shower before I got
to Rells spot. The phone rang again. I
looked at the caller I.D. and the number
had a block on it.
"Hello?"
"So we bangin on each other now?" the
voice asked.
"Look don't be playin on my phone if you

want something just ask!"
"You seriously don't know who I am?"
"Nah, I had a long day. I'm busy so either
talk or stop calling."
"It's Serena, I called cause I wanted to see
you again."
"I told you I'm busy. I'll call you when I'm
able to meet up with you."
"Aight mother fucka I just wanted to see
you don't be actin all funny!" she spat.
"I'm not trying to igg you or anything but I
gotta deal with a lot of stuff right now. My
man was shot and I wanna make sure his
family is all taken care of. I also have to
get people to work and I gotta get in the
shower."
"Aight, call me when you can."
"Aight"

Chapter 17

Before Rell left the crib he made
sure he had the flowers for Mrs. Turner.
He rode most of the way listening to the
radio. The news was saying how the black
minorities continue to be victimized by
Police brutality. Some nigga named
Jermaine got his ass whipped by three
cops. It allegedly was retaliation to the
increase of police deaths. Rell thought of
how Dex offed that police sergeant, shits
becoming a problem. Rell arrived at the
hospital and asked the receptionist for a
room of a Mr. Turner. At the door Rell
seen that Mrs. Turner was asleep and
Blaze was still out, so he slipped in quietly

and left the flowers on the table. He left as quietly as he came and asked the receptionist to inform them that he was there, and then left the hospital. He called Onnie when he got to the car.

"Hello?" Onnie answered.

"Yo, I'm about to go home cause Crock wants to holla at us there. Meet me at the crib in like a half."

"Aight"

Rell was about ten minutes out and called Crock but he received no answer. When he got home he put some food and drinks out so everyone would be accommodated. It took about another ten minutes to have the place the way he wanted before people began to arrive.

"Yo Rell what it is?" Smooth asked as he walked in with a bag with some food in it.

"Aint shit, the game on we can get it in until everyone shows up." They played for about ten minutes when Onnie arrived.

"Yo what's up yall?" He spat.

"Aint shit." They both said.

"I brought some drinks you know Belvie and some Cognac."

"Put them in the kitchen Crock should be here soon." Rell replied.

Onnie went to the kitchen and put the drinks in the fridge. Then went to watch the game. The score was tight, 14-13 Smooth was winning.

"Yo I got next." Onnie claimed.

The door opened slowly and everyone stopped and looked. Rell and

Smooth had their hands on their pistols and waited. Meme and Mel walked in with their hands full.

"Damn! Why yall lookin like that?" Mel screamed.

"We aint know who was opening the door all slow and shit." Rell responded.

"Rell?" Mel called.

"I got you a surprise." And handed him a box. He looked at it and said.

"I got something for you too, it's upstairs."

That was enough to send her flying upstairs. Meme sat and ate some salt less pretzels as she watched them play the game. Rell opened the box to see there were a couple Jerseys in it. He looked excited and put them over the arm of the chair. Upstairs Melanie saw the package with the flowers and candy. She removed the plastic and grabbed the bear and went down stairs. Smooth said,

"Yo you about to go down."

"I don't know the fat lady aint sing yet." Rell said.

"Thank you baby" Mel said as she kissed him.

"Aah" Onnie remarked to the kiss.

"Get yourself a woman and you could get the same treatment." Mel said.

"Damn." He said then there was a knock on the door.

"Yo who is it?" Rell asked.

"It's Buck."

"The door should be open."

Buck walked in with a bottle of Cris.

"A Rell, where the kitchen I'ma put this on chill."

"In through there." He said as he pointed, he didn't look cause this might be the last play of the game. Smooth kept talking shit and Rell choked on a field goal and lost 21-20.

"Damn dog you missed a 30 yarder." Onnie said

"It's cool I'ma get mine back." Rell said jealously.

Crock walked in and when he did he was met by Meme jumping into his arms. She kissed him and put a 76ers hat on his head.

"A what's up Crock?" Rell asked giving dap.

"Yo you aight?" I asked

"Yeah we were waiting for you... there's some drinks and shit on the table."

"A Crock?" Onnie called and started to dig in his pocket and pulled out a knot of money and gave it to me.

"Here go this weeks payment I was able to finish majority of my stash before dude arrested me."

"Aight" I said.

"You was arrested?" Smooth and Rell asked.

"Yeah, he was obvious too."

"So how you gonna go about this now?" Buck asked. "Knowing he may be on your top now."

"I don't know yet. I aint trying to bring heat. I was thinking about trying to air him out." Onnie finished.

"Don't get reckless we don't want you going out like Dex. There's always a way to drop a nigga guard. Shit we can follow that nigga and his partner or I can call Snake you know he fucks with those bombs and shit?"

"Yeah that would be easier." Onnie spat.

"I may have to call him anyway. Look the reason we're here is cause as we all know Blaze was shot by one of the Diplomats. We have word that they go to the Forbidden Rhealm, I have a connect inside and we will find out in a week on how they move."

"We gonna move when the word come?" Buck asked.

"Yeah, but we need to know who we movin on first, can't hit the wrong people."

"Will the connect help with the times they be there?" Rell asked.

"Yeah"

"It's a girl isn't it?" Meme asked.

"Why does it matter?" I asked her.

"Just answer the fuckin question!"

"Yeah it's a woman, they have a way of lowering a mans defenses."

"Oh here." Buck said as he handed me a wad of money then said, "I gotta pick up another sixteen for you from spot."

"Aight we'll handle that later, we need to talk now..."

Chapter 18

"The real reason we're here is cause there's a clique that moves weight up on 66th and Broad." I continued.
"Word is that they would be there late tonight."
I looked at my watch 11:45 then said, "We move now we can catch these niggas with their pants down." Buck was anxious and said,
"I got two flack jackets in the trunk I can pick up three on the way."
"Aight, I got a pump and a u-wop in the car. A Rell you still got the silenced P-90's and that MP5?" I asked.
"Yeah I'll go grab them. I can grab the -K-too." Rell said as he went to the basement.
Onnie pulled out two .50 caliber desert eagles and a .38 special from his boot.
"Is everybody strapped? A Smooth you holdin?"
"Yeah, I got my Berettas and my Glock 17."
"Aight, everyone lets get ready to ride, cause I wanna hit them before they roll. Meme we'll be back soon." My cell began to ring.
"Be careful baby." She said and kissed me.
"Hello?"
"You told me to call when they all come back. It was six of them." The voice confirmed.
"Was they carrying anything?"
"Yeah one had a couple gym bags and

there were two who had on book bags."
"Aight I got you when it's over. You know the meet right?" I asked.
"Yeah Cheltenham malls movie theaters parking lot." the voice assured and hung up.
"Aight, yall we out we gotta move quickly."
As everyone was leaving they went to their cars and readied themselves to leave. As we all drove off we followed Buck to pick up the remaining flack jackets. When we left his crib we turned onto Broad and parked. On the corner of 66th street. It appeared that they were moving shit straight out of the complex. The name of it was The Oak Tree Apartments. I couldn't tell if they had a look out or not. There was a nigga at the door smoking a cigarette.
"Yo they in room B39." I informed them and we all split up. Me and Buck went through the front and Onnie went to the fire escape with Smooth. Rell went in the back entrance. As me and Buck approached this nigga at the door he asked.
"Yall looking for something?"
"Yeah!" I said.
"I'm looking for this nigga." I reached in my jacket and pulled out my silenced 9mm and shot him twice in the chest and once in his head. Buck was already through the door and was on his way up the stairs. He took post and waited as I came up behind him...

Rell seemed to have it easy until he heard some voices over him talking.

"So did you get paid yet?" A deep raspy voice asked.

"Nah I'm waiting to see BJ. He said he had to talk to me."

Rell pulled his two Taurus' and knocked on the door and went down a flight of steps. He heard them open the door and after a minute the door closed.

"Yo I swore I heard something."

"Yeah me too..." the voice was interrupted by the thunder of Rells guns. One of the men was hit in the leg and he fell to the ground. The other tried to run up the stairs and had his braids glued to the wall with a shot through the temple. Rell couldn't see the nigga who fell, although he left a trail of blood through the door. Rell swore the door was closed he opened it and saw the blood turned left. He was becoming more paranoid but he knew he had to kill him. He jumped out of the doorway and shot the first thing he seen on the ground. The nigga who was crawling shot three back and hit Rell twice in the chest. The third bullet hit the wall by his head. Rell focused and shot him in the head. Rell fell to the floor and peeled the vest off his chest. He never felt a bullet kiss his chest before. When the vest cooled he strapped it back on and ran up the stairs. He was startled when he ran into another nigga who was sleep on the door. He pointed his gun and said,

"Get your bitch ass up nigga."
This nigga was so nervous he fell out of
the chair.
"Come on young blood I'm just a
messenger, a watcher. I don't want
anything to do with these niggas." Rell
looked even more angry.
"One thing I despise is a nigga who begs."
He cocked the hammer and asked
"You beggin nigga? Hum, is you beggin?"
the man opened his mouth and before he
got the words out Rell shot him between
his eyebrows. Rell started back up the
stairs...
Me and Buck were at the door to their
floor. Buck asked,
"Who we looking for?"
"These niggas robbed my man "Q" from
N.Y. and he asked for a favor." I said.
"What kill these niggas?"
"Nah I need to get his gym bags." I said
and finished with,
"Yall my fam yall can do what yall want
with the rest. Just don't leave prints."
I turned the beam on and put it on the ear
of one of them niggas standing post. Then
changed my mind.
"Yo follow my lead!"
        I started down the hall and they
looked as I was going down. I caught eye
of the other exit and seen Rell coming
towards us. These niggas didn't even
expect what was about to happen. I pulled
out and shot the first of the two four
times, and Buck unloaded three rounds

into the second man before he fell. We reloaded and called Smooth knowing his cell was on vibrate.

"Hello?"

"Yo we going in now so the first nigga you see lay em down."

"Aight"

Smooth was looking in the window and seen two niggas standing in the kitchen. He signaled Onnie to take the left. As soon as they rushed the window Smooth shot the first in the back three times, and hit the second with four in the chest. Onnie jumped in through the window and let off four shots and hit his target with two in the chest, one of his bullets knocked that nigga throat out...

Hearing the shots I kicked the door in and Rell and Buck rushed through first and shots were fired. I went in and the place seemed secure. Everyone seemed to be settled and there was a cell phone ringing in the closet. This tall slender mother fucka came running out and Buck tackled him at the door. Rell had his gun trained on his head.

"Wait, wait. Hold up don't shoot him yet. Look" I said

"Chances are you a dead man no matter what so you may as well relax." His face was puzzled and shaken.

"Tie this nigga up. Oh! And pull those bodies in from the hallway."

I grabbed the gym bags and called "Q".

"Yo what's up son?"
"It's Crock, I got them niggas you told me of and I got one of them tied up here now. I found your bags and I'll see you in a couple hours."
"Aight son good lookin."
"Aint bout shit I'll see you in a couple."
"Aight"

Despite the blood the place looked rather nice. The sofa was a butta and they had a Persian rug that had stains in it now. There was money stacked on the kitchen table and keys of coke on the dining room table. This was a come up, but I put this nigga in the trunk. Before I left I told them.
"A split that shit up and holla at me tomorrow. Oh Buck be sure there's no prints, so do a sweep when yall leave."
Aight"

Upstairs Smooth and Rell had the money counted up and stacked it in sets of five. It was $250.000 each. There were some guns found in the stove and fridge. There were two automatic pumps and two .44 longs. Buck came in and said,
"Crock said don't be long."

They grabbed their cuts and Rell grabbed Crocks share and threw it in a book bag then grabbed the pumps and they all left their separate ways. Buck was sure to sweep the spot of prints and shell casings. When he felt it was clean he left as well...

Chapter 19

I've been driving for about two hours and seen a rest stop. I pulled in and got some food and filled my tanks. Then got back on the road. Once I got to 149th street I pulled up to the front of Quincy's ducky spot between Amsterdam and Broadway. I called to see if he was in.
"Hello"
"Q" I'm out front with the goods. I said
"You playin." He said and looked out the window and said,
"You aint playin I'll be right down."
The door opened and "Q" walked out with a white T-shirt and a blue Roc a wear jeans. He sported a pair of trees and a du-rag. Quincy stood 5'7" but his name rang bells in Queens like a grandfather clock. We been tight since playing ball against each other at the park. He came up to the window and asked,
"Yo what up B?"
"Aint shit, lets take a ride." I said and he got in.
"That's you?" I said pointing under the seat.
"That's what you asked for right?" I started to drive towards the park. It was dark and we could dispose of that nigga in the trunk.
"See that's why I fucks with you! How'd you get this shit so fast?"

"For my fam I move mountains. Plus I was hoping we could come to terms on moving some of my product out here."

"Damn! All business wit you huh? I don't know shit has been picking up and I wouldn't want anyone to set trip."

We pulled into the park and talked for a while and then there was noise coming from the trunk.

"Yo what's all that about?" he asked looking startled.

"Oh my bad I forgot to tell you, I got one of them niggas in the trunk, and I thought you may wanna see him first."

"Let me see that nigga son!" "Q" spat.

We got out and went to the back, I opened the trunk and the light barley illuminated his face.

"Damn, what the fuck is that smell!" I snapped at him as I dragged him from the trunk.

"This pussy shit himself. That's fucked up! A "Q" is this one of those niggas?" I asked as I looked around noticing it was rather quiet this late in the evening.

"Yeah that's that pussy!" and followed up with a strong right hook that busted his eye open. The punch sent him tumbling into my car.

"Hold up! Hold up!" I stopped him. "Not on my car." I grabbed the dazed man and dragged him behind a tree.

"I told you I play no games when it come to my team. Is you a part of the team?" I asked.

"What kind of question is that?" "Q" asked looking confused,

"Cause my team aint gotta worry about niggas like this cause I get them dealt with fast." "Q" looked stern and watched my every move. I pulled my silenced 9mm and said,

"Look one thing you need not worry about is my loyalty. I'm trying to get in the door and you can help with that."

As I finished I carefully aimed my nine at that nigga head, six shots made a memory of his face. "Q" looked bewildered, he was thinking of how he could plug this young nigga in without ruffling any feathers. Then he thought of 125th and St. Nick. There were some young niggas that moved weight but always had their money fucked up.

"I know of a spot you could move on." "Q" said knowing that them young refugees had more than bad tempers.

"Yeah that's what's up but I know there's a catch aint it?" I asked as I put my nine back in its holster.

"Yeah these young niggas that move my shit are thrown. They aint good for shit." We got in the car and drove back to the spot and we continued to talk. I had to ask him,

"Why would anyone set a bunch of reckless niggas loose on the strip?"

"I figured I could control them and I was proven wrong. I haven't laced them

because they like to drop my opposition."
"Oh like flirting with a double edged sword?"
"Yeah"
"Hold up am I getting this right? I have to either remove them from the strip or I have to put them to work?"
"Yeah but I rather you remove them!" Quincy said with a serious look. I continued to think this might not be worth it. I got Philly on smash and now to flood N.Y. I gotta off more niggas. That shit may come back to bite me in the ass in the long run. I figured "Q" was testing my gangsta, so I let the thought linger.
"Look "Q" I got strong connects in a lot of high places so why can't we put our heads together? I'd hate to step on any toes." I said as I started to roll a blunt.
"I got my shit tight in Killadel so I wanna sell my shit to other heavy hitters."
"That's real good timing cause my last supplier got popped by the DEA last week. Then came home and got rocked by some niggas. Look I need about forty keys by Saturday." "Q" said searching for a reaction.
"I can have it up here on Friday." I said.
"Tomorrow damn, now what's the price on them? Sanchez and Tito sold theirs for 20 a pop."
        Damn they either had a drought or they were killing his pockets.
"Nah I fucks with you, I'll let them go for 18 a key."

"Aight so that's about what seven and some change?"
"Seven twenty." I said doing the math in my head.
"Aight look." "Q" said as he unzipped one of the bags. "Here's three hundred and sixty now, and I'll give your man the rest tomorrow."
He got out and left the bag on the floor on the passenger side.
"Aight. My man will be in a rental, I'll let you know tomorrow what to look for."
"Holla at me tomorrow to let me know the status of everything." He said as we shook hands and parted ways...
Meme and Melanie were watching a movie on Cinimax and Mel came outta the blue with,
"How do you get Crock to make love to you?"
Shocked Meme almost choked on a piece of popcorn. She didn't know let alone understand how to answer her question.
"Umm. I, I don't make him do anything. He has a very insatiable sex drive. It's me who has to keep up with him, usually it's him who asks to make love."
"So you guys don't worry about the other cheating?" Mel asked innocently.
"In order to cheat you have to be an item. I love him dearly but we haven't taken the next step yet."
Mel seemed to really be touched by this situation showing tears and all.
"Maybe you have to set the mood, don't

just lay there like a dead fuck. Put on some soft music and incense. You know put on some lace and dance for him." Mel listened and took in all the advice and asked,

"What if he doesn't like it?"

"If he doesn't like it he's either gay or he has another woman pleasing him."

"I hope it works."

"It will!"

As they were talking about their love lives Rell walked in the house with Smooth and Buck bringing up the rear. Mel acted like they were talking about the movie. Rell went into the kitchen and Buck sat between meme and Mel.

"Where crock at?" Meme asked Buck.

"He had to drop some work off. He'll probably go straight home cause he was looking tired when he left."

"Damn, what yall let Onnie go with him? He don't trust him like that!" she snapped.

"Nah, he told us to handle the mess we made." Smooth said.

"Then if Onnie aint go with him where's Onnie?" Meme asked.

They all looked around but had no luck on finding him, Buck tried to clear his mind of negative thoughts, but there were reasons why he had them. The more he thought of them the more he felt betrayed and concerned for Crock. Smooth broke the silence.

"Yo that nigga missin and he was just booked!"

Buck fought the notions and replied, "That nigga probably got greedy and went back for those guns we left. You know him!"

Buck then called Crock to see what should be done on the situation.

"Yo what is it?" I answered.

"Crock that nigga Onnie missin."

"Wasn't he with Smooth?" Buck looked at Smooth and asked.

"<Yo, wasn't he with you earlier?>"

"<Yeah, but after we split the goods he left to the bathroom and came right back>"

"Smooth said he came back after he went to the bathroom."

"The last time I've seen him was when me and him helped you, I don't remember him after that."

"Shit! This aint good!"

"For who?" Buck asked.

"For both us and him. He could be dead or tied up with them niggas back at the apartments. He could be trying to cut down one of those cops. Worse case he's telling and you know how we deal with that." Letting his imagination linger.

"So what do we do?" Buck asked.

"We aint got much choice but to wait it out. See if he turns up one of two ways." Continuing "alive or dead!"

"Aight, want me and Smooth to check the apartments out?"

"Yeah but remember the cops may be flooded down there."

"Bet. I'll just holla at you tomorrow, and

let you know." Buck said as he hung up. "Crock said to wait it out, me and Smooth are to check out the apartments first."

Buck headed towards the door and Smooth followed. Rell came back from the kitchen.

"Yall out?"

"Yeah"

"Holla at me in the am."

"Aight." Meme watched as they left.

"Mel mind if I stay until Crock come and get me?" she asked.

"Nah girl my house is your house."

Mel started upstairs and told her to lock up with the key on the door.

"I'll get the key from you tomorrow."

"Aight thanks girl."

Meme continued to watch movies and dozed off...

Chapter 20

Waking up to an empty bed was something I became used to. I still wondered where my woman was, so I called her cell. It rung four times and the machine picked up. I hung up and went in the bathroom and washed my face, then brushed my teeth. I figured she could still be at Rells, the clock blinked ten. I still had time to holla at Serena, but decided money before honeys and grabbed my cell and hit Buck up.

"Yo what's poppin?" he answered.

"I need two of P.D.K's finest to make a delivery today."

"When?" Buck asked.

"What you doing now?"

"I'm about to eat this pizza."

"I need you to take forty up to my man "Q"."

"What, by myself?" he asked.

"Take Rell with you I know Smooth went to see his brother."

"Aight I got you!" he said as he hung up.

I drove to see Miranda at the Rhealm. As I crossed the bridge I kept an eye out for that blue Beemer. When I got to the club I seen she was cleaning the bar.

"What's up Gorgeous?" I said with a soft tone.

"Don't let my man hear you say that."

Shocked to hear she had a man I asked, "Damn and who the fuck is your man?!"

"Lil Ron, he coming home from the county today."

"He sounds familiar, what's the verdict with them diplomats?"

Still wiping down the counter she said,

"Wednesday they were talking about some nigga fucking with some bitch who worked in the county Ron in."

"What, they come like everyday?"

"Nah they come on Tuesdays and Wednesday, but they be deep on Fridays, Oh the one you call Razor must be the leader of their team cause they all listen to

him."
"What this nigga look like? Anything that would set him apart from the others."
"Yeah he wears a eye patch over his left eye and he has two tear drops on his right eye. The first time I seen him he only had one. I don't know what they mean."
"Look I'ma holla at you later aight? You a member of P.D.K. now welcome to the family."
"Thanks Crock it's nice to be a part of a family."
      I left the bar and sat in the car. Then decided to call my man Snake.
"Speak!" he answered.
"It's Crock you got a second?"
"Yeah what's the situation?"
"I need you to give someone a present for me. He drives a blue Beemer with mirror tint."
"Where and when?"
"The Forbidden Rhealm, tonight."
"Consider it done." As our lines cut I made sure that I drove to the hospital to check on Blaze since I was in the area...
      Smooth was holding his mother as she cried.
"I can't believe I lost another baby I can't lose you, you my last."
Remembering his younger brother Terrance who was hit by a car eight years ago.
"I aint going no where mom." Smooth said trying to ease his mom's pain.
"Bennie was only 24, he was too young to

die." The doctor came in and said, "I'm sorry Mrs. Turner but we have more disturbing news."

"What!" Smooth snapped at him.

"Your sons' health insurance policy was nullified as of a year and a half ago."

"So what you saying doc?" Smooth Questioned.

"Since the policy was cut the bill will have to be paid by the family of the deceased."

"How much we talking here doc?" she asked.

"The subtotal is around six thousand four hundred dollars."

"I'll have it here tomorrow."

"I must say I'm sorry for your loss..."

I walked in as the doctor was leaving. I knew something was going on cause they were still holding each other.

"Crock, this nigga said we gotta pay the cost out of our pockets."

"Why?"

"His health insurance stopped a year ago."

"Damn! Will you be able to take care of it?" I asked.

"Yeah"

"I gotta handle something so call me if you need anything. But for now you need to be with your family."

"Aight"

I left the hospital and got in the car. I thought I haven't hollered at Serena in a minute so I called her.

"Hello?"

"You busy?" I asked her.

"Nah I got some free time if you up to it."
"Just come to my crib I live on Morton
street the fifteen hundred block by the
school."
"I'll be there in about twenty minutes."
"Aight I'll leave the door open for you, I
just got out the shower and I'm still hot."
        I started the car and followed the
directions to her spot. I began thinking of
what Miranda was saying, almost an hour
ago.
"<That nigga you call Razor wears an eye
patch.>"
"He must be the leader of their little
organization." I'ma have Snake dead that
nigga...
        Sitting in a booth at Italianos' Buck
started eating a slice of pizza when his cell
rang then stopped. Laying it on the table
by his soda he looks up at his hearts own
and said,
"I have to handle some business today."
She looked at him with a distant stare of
concern. Knowing what she says will be
irrelevant.
"I understand." Was all she could muster
up to say. She's been with Buck for almost
four years now. Even before he pledged to
the P.D.K. clique. Although he knew Crock
and Rell for about ten years. She also
knows not to intervene with his business
from past experiences. The sordid memory
still pierces as though it was only
yesterday's news.
...Two years back she interrupted Buck

and Dex in a transaction with some vicious niggas. Not knowing a set up, was entangled with them now.

"Yo you got my money? Said the Jamaican known as Kas.

"Yeah it's right here." Dex said and tossed the bag to his feet.

"That's good what else you got for me?" He hissed. Confused Buck lashed out with.

"The fuck talking about nigga?" as he reached in his coat. Then felt the barrel of a gun at the back of his head.

"Don't be foolish." The voice spoke from behind him.

"What's taking so fucking long?" Jasmine said as she got out of the car unsure of the situation. The man lowered the gun to Bucks back.

" Get back into the car!" Buck yelled.

" No! I'm tired of you always…." She was snatched up by one of the Jamaicans before she could finish her sentence.

" Get the fuck off me!" she squealed. They let Dex go cause they always done business together. Not realizing he took it personal. "Good look." Dex yelled.

Buck looked back before he was stuffed into the truck with his girl. Buck told himself "if he was ever going to see Dex alive he'd kill him for setting him up!" They drove for awhile then pulled into an alley. They went into an old apartment and threw Buck into a chair and tied him down. Kas then took his girl over to the couch and asked Buck.

" So what you think this pretty flower wurt to you mon?" Buck igged him thinking to himself, looking at his henchman Kas said.

"This rude boy got some nuts, let cut tem off and feed the dogs with tem."

He then caressed Jasmines lips.

"You touch her again and I'll kill you!" Buck snapped as he threw his gaze at the Jamaican. There wasn't a response from him. Buck watched intently as Kas threw Jasmine across the couch and snatched her clothes off til nothing covered her body and told her to open her mouth. When she refused he slapped her face and repeated his question.

"Open your mout!" This time she complied and fondled her mouth with the gun.

"You like that don't you?"

"Look don't involve her do what you want with me. Let her go."

"You mean touch her like this?" he said as he grabbed at her tits and ass. She struggled to free herself from the grip and was struck across the face again. He continued his assault and Buck yelled.

"What are you doing this for?" the henchmen punched Buck in the jaw and said,

"Shut the fuck up and watch the show!" Then they taped his mouth shut. Kas began to strip until he was naked. Jas knowing what was about to happen braced herself.

"This for my brother and his girl you killed back in 03. we knew we'd catch you slippin." He finished his statement and started stroking his dick in front of Jasmine. She tried to scramble free once more and was grabbed by the big Jamaican. He threw her on her back and rammed himself into her. Helpless all she could do is let out a yelp. Finding his stroke he continued for fifteen minutes, which felt like an eternity to Jasmine. Kas looked back at Buck now and then to relish the look on his face. Buck was so stricken that he did something he hadn't done since he was eleven. He cried! Feeling helpless, ashamed and betrayed he prayed she would be okay. Kas kept pumping through his assault trying to dig and shred her vaginal walls for life. He then flipped her over and fucked her in the ass with no lube. Jasmine never had anal before which made the pain all that much more unbearable. She was so numb from the pain all she could do was cry cold silent tears. Kas enjoyed the fact that Buck was helpless bound and gagged. He was nearing his limit and pumped faster in her tight little hole. Buck looked around with tears in his eyes and found his own sense of gratification to see two dots on the other two Jamaicans heads. He didn't understand, then he heard something like a cough and they fell. Kas who was too close to his own climax to respond as he normally would. Dex appeared from the kitchen and Crock from the front letting two shots rip through Kas knees as he nutted on himself. Dex cut Buck loose as I tried to cover Jasmine with my coat. She threw me aside and began to kick Kas in the face and when he tried to cover up she kicked him in his neck. Buck asked Dex. "What was that all about? You came back and I love you for that, but you were too late."

"Look I don't know why they cut me loose." Dex said

"I went and grabbed Crock out of bed and we rushed back."

Buck took the gun off the T.V. where Kas left it and shot Kas in the legs again. Then they walked over to his helpless body with the guns drawn.

"Go ahead bitch ass nigga! I seen everything but judgment anyway. Plus I fucked your bitch she'll always remember me."

I pointed my gun at his head waiting for Buck to give the word. Before I could blink Jas ripped the gun from me and unloaded seven shots into him. Kas' body began to twitch and shake then Buck shot three rounds into his head which ceased his movement. Buck took his girl upstairs to find some clothes and get dressed. He wanted to take her home to get her cleaned up. I walked over to them and said,

"Before yall do anything she should go to the hospital. Cause you don't know what

he had!"
"Aight"
Just call the cops and let them know you were raped and you managed to grab his gun and shot him." Dex said
"Jas, only if your comfortable with it!" I said.
"You sure?" she asked.
"Ma, you've been through a lot, but if you do just call us when you get to the hospital."
"Aight"
That was the last day they stayed in Jersey, they picked up and moved to Philly. They never looked back...

Chapter 21

Knock, knock, knock as Buck knocked on the door.
"Who is it?" Mel asked
"Buck."
The door unlocks and opens, Melanie was standing in a night gown and said
"Rells in the kitchen" Buck walked in and said
"What's up Mel?" Then headed to the kitchen.
"You aight in here?" Buck asked. Rell standing in his slippers and shorts over the stove cleaning.
"What's up nigga?" Rell asked.
"We need to handle some B.I. today."
"When?" Rell asked, stopping what it was

he was doing.

"When you put your clothes on!"

"Aight where we going?"

"N.Y. Crock wants us to drop off and pick up."

"How much?"

"Forty and three sixty." Buck said.

"Aight." Rell walked out to get dressed, Buck went into the living room and watched the T.V. hearing someone coming down the stairs Buck looked up and seen Meme.

"A what up Meme?"

"Nothin" really where Crock at?"

"He still at the hospital I guess." Buck answered

"What you about to do?" She asked

"Crock asked me to handle something."

Seeming to show little interest, she walked to the kitchen. "Looking good as always" he said himself as he watched her strut to the kitchen. Not seeing Rell come down he just stared.

"You ready nigga?!" Rell spat snapping Bucks heads off Memes apple bottom.

"Yeah my bad." Buck said

"For what she aint my girl, you'd have to apologize to Crock if he caught you gawkin' at his girl."

"Nah it aint even like that. I wouldn't even disrespect my man like that." Buck said.

"Whatever nigga just don't slip again."

They both left to pick up the rental in Rells car. After picking out their car they grabbed the product from the spot and started their two hour drive. On the radio the news was saying something about an inmate who stabbed a guard.

<"This tragic incident, inmate Latrel Stevens was found guilty of first degree manslaughter and inciting a riot. He was sentenced to seven and a half to twenty three years running concurrent to his juvenile life plus two years probation.">

Rell began to think, it's about time they expand south or hiring more clientele. He wanted to holla at Crock to see what he thought. Pulling into a rest stop Buck ran to grab some food and soda. Rell filled the tank with gas and waited for Buck to come back then rolled out. While in the car Buck asked,

"You got your Glock on you?"

"Yeah why?"

"I'm taking off my safeties."

"Oh yeah can never be too safe."

Another ten minutes of driving and they rolled up to 148th and Broadway. Before turning down Amsterdam Rell called Crock.

"Yo what's up?"

"Yo we about to holla at that nigga "Q". call him and let him know we be outside in a second."

"Aight give me a minute..."

as they looked down the street they seen someone come outside and stand on the stoop with a gym bag.

"That must be him." Rell suggested.

"Yeah lets go." Buck replied.

Turning down Amsterdam Rell drove up cautiously. Watching for any sudden movements. When they pulled up to the spot, "Q" looked down and nodded. Rell and Buck nodded in acknowledgement. "Q" walked up to the car with the bag followed by his two cronies.
"Here's the three sixty as promised with a little extra for your struggles."
Buck didn't respond to the gesture but Rell said,
"Look dog! No disrespect but we can't take this!" snatching the money from Buck that was thrown on his lap, then handed it back.
"Crock takes care of this team, I'm sure you understand." Rell finished.
"I feel you son, it's all love." Rell then gripped the bags from the back seat and handed them to Buck who in turn handed them out to the cronies.
"There's your forty, Oh Crock said holla at him when you can."
"Aight, yall sure yall don't want anything? I got drinks inside, we got weed and I got these bitches about to put on a show." "Q" said with a little smirk barely noticeable.
"Nah my man! We gotta go, we got a schedule to keep to" Buck said.
"Aight youngins be safe."
    "Q" turned and grabbed a fine ass Italian chick and made his way to the door. Rell told Buck,
"You never take extra anything from a nigga you supplying."

"Why?"

"It's a rule of thumb and it's bad for business, plus they'll think you owe them a favor later."

"Aight. My fault." Rell pulled off and begun their long ass trip back to Philly...

Smooth still feeling the pain of losing his brother decided to ask Crock for some work to help pay for some of the funeral expenses. Knowing Crock might help anyway. He just wanted to feel he was pulling his own weight. Stepping out of the crib and looking up and down the street he seen that the block seemed rather busy. He didn't know who that nigga Prince worked for but if he was to start pulling his weight he was gonna to press that nigga to find his supplier. Starting his car Smooth felt his cell vibrating.

"Hello!" he answered as he drove down the street.

"Hey baby is everything okay?" recognizing the voice to be Tameka.

"Yeah I'm keeping myself above water. How are you today?"

"I'm okay are we still going out to eat after the movie?"

"Yeah I just gotta holla at Crock real quick."

"Are you on your way cause I don't wanna miss the matinee."

"I'm five minutes out."

"Aight bay."

Smooth pulled up to a red light and called Crock, but couldn't get through.

Turning down 8th and Diamond Smooth stopped at a corner house and beeped the horn twice. The door opened and out walked Tameka with a black dress that fit her body perfectly. She had on a little jewelry. But she had a ring that was a gift from Smooth a year ago. It's a six karat canary diamond with ten one karat topaz gems in the shape of a heart around it. With her Hispanic decent her hair was long and wavy down to her lower back. "Damn you look good!" he said as she stepped into the car. She leaned over and gave him a kiss. That's when he smelled the enticing perfume it was that Channel shit he bought her for Valentines Day. "You don't look bad yourself." Meka replied with a lustful and inviting tone. "I got on a tuxedo, it's just like a suit. You seen me in a suit before. You on the other hand, you tryin to start some shit, aint you?" as he voiced his opinions. "I gotta look good for my man don't I?" stroking his ego as her accent began to kick in as she spoke. "Come on honey stop talking to me like that, before we miss the show." As they drove off he knew he got his point across cause she didn't respond. While driving Luther came on the radio, Smooth didn't say anything but he noticed she kept glancing over at him. She'd turn back if he looked and he couldn't figure why she was doing it so he came out with it. "Something..." They said simultaneously.

"Go head baby I can wait." He said
"No, No, you go , I still don't know how to
put it together yet." She said as she looked
down at her stomach.
"Put what together" he said "I was
wondering if I done something wrong?"
"Why would you think that?" knowing
from woman's intuition what he was
referring to.
"Look" he said sternly. "You know I love
you right?"
"Of course I do. Where you going with
this?" she asked confused.
"I was thinking about working with Crock
to fill in for Blaze. Onnie's no where to be
found and Buck is working with two tone
and ant around the clock." Meka spoke
little but her emotion was expressed
through her facial expression. He knew
her concern.
"Don't look like that! You know we will
need the money to pay for the crib and
plus we gotta pay for the funeral. I'm not
taking anymore handouts. I wanna work
for mines."
"beta buku trabajo!" speaking Spanish. "I
mean a real job?" she spat as the tears
welded up in her eyes and ran down her
cheeks. When he seen this he wiped the
tears and said,
"I'll be careful I promise. Don't cry, please
don't cry." He parked the car in the lot and
cut it off.
"You know I was headed in that direction."
"That's not why I'm crying."

"then why shed them?"
"Because I'm pregnant! I'm with child Steven! Your child."
"What?!" flooded with emotion he couldn't think straight.
"When?!"
"It's true I found out two weeks ago. Now you wanna put your life in the hands of those P.D.K. niggas. For what? A few extra dollars. You know when you're **IN**! The only way out is death. Be it yours or be it another's!"
"Don't look at me that..." cutting him off Meka said,
"Don't look at you like this! My child will need his father, how would I tell your child as a teen his father was a petty drug dealer?" slipping in a sly remark.
"You don't, you make something up."
　　Understanding he made his mind up Tameka wiped her face and got out of the car. Smooth felt guilty for ruining her supposed perfect evening...

Final Chapter!

"Holla"
"Yeah he's here with his team!"
"Aight I'm up the street, I need you to watch them."
"Aight"
　　"Ring, Ring"
"Yo!"
"They here where you at?"

"I'm in route, I got enough to drop half a block."

"Good that's real good. Just don't be too eager we gotta do this right!"

"You're the boss!"

Pulling up to Jefferson street Rell turned onto 17th and signaled Ant to come over.

"What up Rizel?"

"Take this to the crib."

"Aight"

Buck got out the car and went to his usual spot and started to sell some work. Rell started to ride off when Two-Tone called him.

"Rell?!" running over to the car.

"Yo"

"You see Crock today?"

"Nah why?"

"Some nigga was around the end like an hour ago claiming he know him."

"How he know you?"

"He didn't he knew Ant I think."

"That's the first problem. Thinking! You don't think you act." Rell said sarcastically. "What he say his name was?"

"Oz. he said he worked for a nigga named E out D.C..."

"Oh aight he must want a re-up."

"I don't know."

"I'll take care of that, just get that money and watch each others backs out here."

Rell left and went to the rental spot to drop the car off. He got in his wheel and called Crock. The phone rang three times and then he heard,

"Yo..."

"A I gotta holla..." Rell stopped as he was cut off by,

"I'm busy at this time so if you repeat what you said after the tone, I'll get back to you. Beep..."

"<Yo I hate that shit dog. Some nigga named Oz was down here for E saying something. I didn't get the whole jest of it. Holla at me when you get a chance...>"

Rell drove to the crib to chill a bit...

Bucks been outside for a couple hours and decided shit was slow enough for him to put the money up and go home. Ant and Two-Tone handled their shit and already left the block. Buck called a cab as he put the money up. Crock aint like the young niggas hustling too late cause that was Bucks, Onnie's, and Blazes job, his generals. He didn't voice it but he and everyone else knew Rell is his right hand. They never really expected to move up in the chain cause shit was tight. After Buck finished washing his hands he grabbed his jacket and left knowing old head Kenny was upstairs. Buck got in the cab and went somewhere he hadn't been in a couple days. Opening the door he could tell that Jasmine was home cause it smelled like food.

"Jas?! You home?"

"Yeah I'm in the kitchen. I cooked your favorite." She said like she wasn't angry with him anymore.

"Fried chicken, stuffed peppers, yellow rice and green beans. To top it off I made some ice cold Kool aid."

"Damn, you throwin down huh?" he said as he walked in the kitchen to see his woman standing by the chair with a sexy ass negligee on. He walked over and kissed her and sat down.

"I got another surprise for you in the bedroom." Buck hating to disappoint really wasn't up for throwing down tonight, he was exhausted...

sitting about two car lengths from the Beemer I just watched as Snake made his way to the car. When he got there he disappeared for a few seconds and appeared just as fast. He walked up towards me and kept going as if nothing happened or his car was in that direction. I then got out and walked into the club. The place was packed, the stools at the bar were filled and three of the four private booths were occupied. Miranda seemed to be filling in for a waiter or waitress cause she was serving drinks. I intercepted her on her way back to the bar.

"Hey Ma, what's the deal?" I asked looking at the drunk faces at the bar.

"Busy, very busy!"

"Look I was gonna holla at you later but has your man come to see you yet?"

"Yeah why?" she asked as she made her way to another table with a tray of drinks. I followed her and continued with,

"I just wanted to know if he was looking for work."

 "I don't know ask him yourself." She said laying the drinks down.

"I will when I meet him." She then kissed this nigga sitting in one of the chairs.

"Yo what the fuck!" I snapped

"She got a man nigga! Back the fuck up for you get hit the fuck up!" I spat grabbing my Glock.

"Stop it! Calm down Crock. This is my man." She said grabbing my hands somewhat hysterical.

"Oh shit! My bad fam I didn't know." I said then sat with him and his man who said, "You shouldn't pull guns if you don't intend to use them!"

"You right just be thankful yall do know her."

Lil Ron looking at his man like shut the fuck up man this nigga legit.

"I see you that nigga who was looking out for her when I was down." Lil Ron said.

"Yeah she good people, plus she a member."

"A member of what!?" he asked as he looked up at her.

"P.D.K." I said.

"Them niggas deep we heard all about them in the county. One of them killed like four people and a cop."

"Look I'm tryin to put you on. If you looking for work?" I said

"What kind of work?" His fat ass homie asked.

"Yo who the fuck are you! I'm talking over here."

"A fat cat fall back man we don't want any problems with this man he offerin us work." Lil Ron said.

"Look I think you smart enough to know what kind of work I'm offering." I said back at Lil Ron.

"This kind of work will put about eight hundred in your pocket after I take mine off the top."

"You bullshittin?" Lil Ron said unconvinced.

"There's a few things you'll learn I don't do. I don't tolerate disrespect." Glancing out the corner of my eye at Fat-Cat. "I don't play with that money and I definitely don't bullshit."

"Aight" Lil Ron said as Miranda chimed in with.

"How do you think I got this bangin ass job?" seeing he was interested I continued. "Once you a member you die a member. You and your girl will be in a strong team of soldiers. Plus you'd never have to worry about being hungry, ever!"

"I'm in but where you want me to set up?"

"Set up where you feel comfortable, if you see another nigga pushin near or around your strip let me or Rell know and it will be handled."

"Bet."

As I finished up I seen Razor rolling out with like four niggas with him. They all had bandanas on their left biceps. I figured this was my chance to kill two birds with one stone.

"A Lil Ron you and your man roll wit me right Quick."

"Aight"

"Yall drivin or yall together?"

"I drove" Fat-Cat said.

"Aight. I want yall to see something. Fat-Cat get the car and you roll with me Lil Ron."

We all got up and left the club I got to my car and Snake was there with something in his hand. Without saying a word he just handed me the remote.

"Just press when ready and be at least four car lengths back." As he finished whispering he disappeared into the night. I got in and then Lil Ron got in the passenger side. We followed the Beemer on the way to Philly.

"I don't know you that well but I can fuck wit you cause you fuckin with Miranda. The reason you are here is cause there are some things you need to know. I'm lenient when it comes to how you get rid of my product but have my money right before the end of the week. This nigga here in that Beemer fucked up and I hate being played." Slowing to a stop to create a space between us. "They played with that money so I'ma play with their lives." I pulled out the remote and Lil Ron looked confused.

"What's that?"

"This is what happens to those who play

with my money!"

Pressing the button...**BOOM!!**
"Damn. Dog what the fuck!" he said jumping and squirming in the seat as the car exploded. I opened his door and handed him a small package. He was getting out and I said,
"You're a member of P.D.K. now! And tossed him a pager.
"My peoples will be in touch." He left and rolled out with Fat-Cat stricken with shock and disbelief.

I drove past the debris and figured it's time for a little break. I went to the airport and bought a ticket to Miami. The departure time was 2:30 am and it was only ten minutes to two. I sat in the lounge and my cell rang. It was Meme; if I answer and tell her I was leaving I'd never live it down. I waited until the phone stopped ringing and called Rell.
"Hello?"
"Yo it's heated up here in Jersey, feel me? I handled that nigga Razor on the way to Philly. Look I gotta go down Miami for a minute, so I'ma need you and Buck to hold shit down until I come back."
"What you want me to tell Meme?" he asked
"Don't tell her anything give her some money and tell her I needed to disappear for a few."
"And if she aint tryin to hear it?"
"Make her understand, I trust you can do this that's why I called you."

"Aight but what if some shit pops off per say?"

"I will buy a pager or cell then call you with the number for emergencies. Emergencies only give the number to Buck and Meme too."

"Aight family be safe out there."

"For sure."

Hanging up the phone the airline announced my plane was now boarding. While getting on I showed the stewardess my stub and she pointed to my row and returned my stub. I sat down thinking of how Onnie disappeared. That's some weird shit. A different stewardess asked if I needed a pillow. I took it and finally went to sleep...

To be continued...

Brief Epilogue

There's a whole nother world out there that most niggas never experience. "The Game" to truly understand the life and struggles of a made man, you have to be willing to grind all hours of the day. Sacrifice the luxury of nice things in order to flip your shit. You need to keep your ears to the street and have a loyal team behind you riding hard...

David X. Austin

"Special Preview"
"Struggles of a made man"
"The Struggle Continues"

Prologue

So we meet again, I hope you were fortunate enough to have read the prequel to this riveting story you're about to experience. This sequel will take you on a journey through the streets of Philly, B-More, D.C., and New York. Will P.D.K. be able to handle the onslaught of West Virginia and D.C.? There is one way you can find out, and it all begins on the next page...

"<There's been an increase in the murder rate in Philly since the 90's. last year there was an explosion on the New Jersey turnpike that claimed the lives of four individuals. The investigation was put off duc to lack of evidence at the scene...>"

"Damn!" Buck said as the news was going off.

"The game is different now, never know who you really dealing with. Seems to be a potential cop on every corner, the way niggas gettin booked."

"Yeah what can you do? That's the risk we have to take to get this money." Smooth said.

"We own damn near half the city so if niggas start talking word will eventually get back to us. All we have to do is lay back and listen."

"Yeah shit has been real smooth for us which I'm happy about. A when Crock say he was coming back?" Smooth asked as he was changing the channel.

"I don't know you'd have to holla at Rell about that."

"When are yall getting off your asses to do something?" Tameka snapped as she was coming down the steps.

"Stop with all that noise, one of the perks of our jobs is we make money while sitting down."

Tameka sat on the couch and said, "Sounds like yall got lazy since Crock disappeared."

"Nah we got a few young niggas movin out right now." Smooth said as he was still flicking through the channels.

"I wonder what he's been up to for almost a year in the south." Buck said walking towards the window.

"I don't know but we need to holla at that nigga "E" from D.C.!" Smooth said as he began to rub his girl's feet.

"Why what's up?" Buck asked turning from the window.

"Remember we had beef about some money a month ago?"

"Oh yeah"

"After that I put them niggas Mil and Streetz up there in B-more to keep an eye open, and build their cred for future references. Cause you never know when we may have to drop him." Smooth said.

"Crock know about that?" Buck asked

"Nah I haven't had time to bring it up to him." Both Buck and Tameka looked at Smooth like he was joking. Buck broke the silence with

"You know this could bite us in the ass if "E" thinks we tryin him." Buck said as he looked back at the window.

"They got it plus if anything pops off they'll call." Smooth said with confidence.

"Yeah...I hope so!"

"Why you keep looking out the window? What you paranoid?" Tameka said jokingly.

"I aint scared of shit and don't forget that shit!" Buck snapped his head from the window to show he was serious, and continued. "I was wondering who this nigga was down the street with that black nova."

"Where?!" Smooth asked getting up from the couch to see, as they looked out the window there were two men both who looked small in stature and they had two other niggas sitting on the nova. Smooth identified one as Prince a youngin he had issues with before, the other three he didn't know. They bumped into this team on a few occasions and thought nothing of them. They were testing the patients of the older more experienced team, even they weren't prepared for what was gonna happen to them in the near future...

"Nah I don't know the two on the car the light skinned dude's name is Prince."

"Aight I'll check their plate when I go past cause I gotta check them niggas Crock put on."

"Who Lil Ron and Fat Cat?"

"Yeah they should be finished by now, Oh yeah "Q" called for another thirty." Buck said.

"Aight I'll go to the spot to get everything together."

"Aight dog, I'll see you and Meka!" Buck said while leaving the crib. As he got in the car he glanced down the street to see the group getting larger. Thinking to himself he wondered who these niggas were to be forming a crowd on the block. "THA GR8 1" was what the plate said and as he drew closer the plate stated they were from D.C. he knew they weren't visiting. He drove past and headed to Jersey to collect from Lil Ron and Fat-Cat...

"Yo what you need?" Mil said to the buyer known as Tank.

"I need fifteen or twenty."

"I got twenty for you but I need to see the money first." When he finished he pulled his cell and waited to hear Tanks response.

"Aight!" he said and looked back at his dark SUV. The door opened and out stepped a short Asian chick with long black hair. She had a silver briefcase hand cuffed to her waist. She walked over with the elegance of a model and her body was curvy for an Asian. She held the case out and tank opened it revealing 6 rows of 60 thousand.

"Aight" Mil said as he checked the bills.

"It's all good, hold up." he said then dialed a number and waited for an answer.

"Yo"

"A Streetz bring twenty up for me."

"Aight here I come." As Mil finished the call he looked at his watch.

"Everything copastetic?" Tank asked.

"Yeah he's coming now with it."

Tank uncuffed the briefcase and handed it to Mil. After taking the case a grey celebrity rolled up and Streetz stepped out.

"Here go your work cuz."

Once again Tank gestured to the SUV and another Asian broad came out. They both grabbed the gym bags from Streetz and went back to the car.

"I hope to do business with you again sometime." Tank said as he got into the wheel and rolled out.

"A what up cuz?" Streetz asked

"Aint shit tryin to handle this B.I. here take this back to the crib for me."

"A you hear that nigga "E" mad cause his shit aint movin like it was."

"So fuck that nigga! He good as dead anyway fuckin with P.D.K." Mil responded.

"You right! Look I gotta holla at this pretty young thing in downtown B-more. Just call me if you need. Streetz said as he was getting in the car.

"Aight fam, I need to relax anyway. I might go to a bar or a club." As their conversation ended Mil got into his LS 400 and rolled down the ship...

"A Ron!" yelled Buck. "Come here right quick."

Ron knew he was short a couple hundred so he took it from his own stash to make it right. It's obvious Fat-Cat was trimming him. He strolled over to Buck and extended his fist for a dap.

"What up my nigga?" showing respect.

"Aint shit, look you got that for me?" Buck said getting right to the point.

"Yeah" handing him a wad of cash, ruffling through the bills Buck was satisfied it was all there. He gave Ron a bag and told him.

"Be sure to keep in touch. Oh! Watch out for SUV's with VA. plates. And where that nigga Fat-Cat?"

"He probably at the spot, you hear from Crock yet?"

"What you worried about him for?" Buck snapped.

"He told me to let him know if we have any problems with another strip. These niggas reppin D.C. hard screamin Dip set and shit"

"Dip set! Aight I'll let him know."

"A let him know they suppose to be movin for some nigga named "E" out D.C."

"How you know?" Buck asked.

"You'd be surprised what bitches know when the money comes out."

"Aight lil nigga you on point, holla if you hear anything else." Buck drove off and paged Crock to hit his cell. Then went to Italiano's to grab some food for him and Jas...

www.ingramcontent.com/pod-product-compliance
Lightning Source LLC
Chambersburg PA
CBHW051924240626
47153CB00004B/1352